Praise for Amanda Grace

In Too Deep

"Honest and constantly interesting."
—*Kirkus Reviews*

But I Love Him

"Ann and Connor inhabit every shade of hope, despair, confusion, ecstasy, longing, rage and guilt with heartbreaking realism…powerful and compulsively readable."
—*Kirkus Reviews*

"Beautifully written and wholly believable…This novel is a departure for Grace—who has written light, frothy tween novels under the name Mandy Hubbard—and marks her as a voice to watch in YA fiction."
—*Booklist*

"Intense. Scary. Heartbreaking. *But I Love Him* is a hard story to read, but one that needs to be told."
—*The Story Siren*

"*But I Love Him* is haunting, heartbreaking, and full of wondrous hope."
—*Sacramento Book Review*

"All I want to do is pretend nothing is wrong
and avoid it all, for eternity, but I know I can't."

Sam is in love with her best friend Nick, but she can't seem
to tell him. So she decides to flirt with golden-boy Carter
Wellesley, hoping Nick will see it and finally realize his true
feelings for her. Although Sam is humiliated by Carter's
cruel rejection of her, it doesn't seem to matter once Nick
confesses he's been falling for her for months.

Yet on Monday, everyone at school is saying that
Carter raped Sam. He didn't, but Sam can't find the words
to tell the truth. Worst of all, she's afraid she'll lose Nick if
he finds out what really happened.

As graduation approaches, Sam discovers that living the
lie isn't as easy as her new friends make it sound—and telling
the truth might be even worse.

IN
TOO
DEEP

For my parents, who raised me to believe I could be anyone I wanted to be. I love you both, and your support means everything.

IN
TOO
DEEP

amanda grace

flux ™
Woodbury, Minnesota

First Edition
First Printing, 2012

Book design by Bob Gaul
Cover design by Ellen Lawson
Cover image © Ron Nickel/Design Pics Inc./Photolibrary Group Inc.

Flux, an imprint of Llewellyn Worldwide Ltd.

This is a work of fiction. Names, characters, places, and incidents are either the product of the author's imagination or are used fictitiously, and any resemblance to actual persons living or dead, business establishments, events, or locales is entirely coincidental. Cover model used for illustrative purposes only and may not endorse or represent the book's subject.

Library of Congress Cataloging-in-Publication Data
Grace, Amanda.
  In too deep / Amanda Grace.—1st ed.
    p. cm.
  Summary: Trying to make her best friend Nick jealous, high school senior Sam becomes involved in a terrible lie that spirals out of control.
  ISBN 978-0-7387-2600-7
  [1. Conduct of life—Fiction. 2. Honesty—Fiction. 3. Rumor—Fiction. 4. High schools—Fiction. 5. Schools—Fiction.] I. Title.
  PZ7.G75127In 2012
  [Fic]—dc23
                                                      2011028806

Flux
Llewellyn Worldwide Ltd.
2143 Wooddale Drive
Woodbury, MN 55125-2989
www.fluxnow.com

Printed in the United States of America

Acknowledgments

Many thanks to my editor, Brian, for being such a blast to work with. Now that this book is done, maybe I'll finally finish that starburst wrapper dress. Thank you, as well, to Sandy, for taking messy drafts and making them sparkle. I'm not sure what I'd do without your sharp eye! And thank you to the rest of the Flux team, especially Courtney and Steven, for being so great to work with.

Thank you to Super Agent Zoe, who has been in every acknowledgment I've ever written because I'll always be indebted to her. And to Jennifer and Saundra, for reading an early draft of *In Too Deep* and talking me off the ledge. You girls rock. I must also thank Taryn Albright, for reading this book on a moment's notice and providing such wonderfully insightful comments.

Lastly, thank you to my husband, who is taking our wonderful (and energetic!) daughter "on an adventure" as I type this, ensuring I don't miss my deadline. Thanks for all you do.

"Oh what a tangled web we weave, when first we practice to deceive."

—Sir Walter Scott

One

Clise your eyes."

"What? Why?" Nick Davis, my best friend, gives me a freaked-out look that makes me laugh. He really is too easy to shock.

I lean back into the buttery-leather bucket seat of Nick's Mustang. "Just do it."

He lets out a big exasperated sigh and closes his eyes, leaning his head back against the headrest. I grab my backpack out of the back seat and unbutton my pants, glancing out into the darkened night. A group of girls pass by, their feet crunching the gravel not far from Nick's car, their giggles breaking the silence. They're heading toward the glowing house in the distance. There's no way anyone can see me, but it still makes me nervous.

When he hears the zipper of my jeans, his eyes pop open.

I scramble to cover up my new lace-trimmed underwear. "No peeking! Geez!"

He squeezes his eyes shut as butterflies swarm my stomach. I can't believe I'm going to change in front of him. If his eyes pop open while my pants are off, I'll never forgive him.

"What are you doing?

"Changing." I struggle to pull my jeans off in the cramped front. This seemed easier in my head. Thank God for the darker-than-dark tint on his windows, because I'm still struggling to untangle the jeans from my ankles, panic welling up.

"Why?" His voice sounds weird, kind of breathy. My heart flutters before I force it back under control.

"It's not like I could walk out of the house in what I wanted to wear." I pull the skirt out of my backpack and slip my bare feet into it, then shimmy it up over my hips. When the zipper on the side slides up, Nick peeks again, one eye at first, then both flare so wide it's like one of those cartoons where the wolf's eyes pop out of his head.

My heart goes *kerthunk* this time. Maybe I should have thought of dressing like this sooner, dressing more like Reyna, his on-again, off-again girlfriend.

Right now, I'm pretty sure they're on again. To my utter, heart-crushing disappointment.

He looks outraged. "What the hell is that?"

I roll my eyes and try to pretend it's no big deal. "It's called a skirt."

"That is *not* a skirt. That is a Band-Aid."

I snort. "You know as well as I do that Carter won't take a second look at me if I'm dressed the same as always."

I think he flinches when I say "Carter." I also think I've imagined it. This is the game in my head every time I'm around Nick these days. The "does he, doesn't he" game. I hate it. And tonight it ends.

I realized I loved Nick the first time I saw him with Reyna, watched the way his lips curled upward when he looked at her, saw his eyes sparkle in a way they never did when it was just us two. And as she trailed her fingers down his arm, laughing flirtatiously, I realized I didn't want to be "just friends" with him anymore, but by then it was too late.

Now all I ever do is watch them break up and get back together and break up and get back together and I can never seem to tell him how I feel. So I've enacted Plan B. I'll make him think something's going on with Carter Wellesley, the world's biggest flirt, and once I see Nick's reaction, I'll finally know if he could ever see me like he sees Reyna. If maybe he could be more than just my best friend, my next-door neighbor.

He pulls the key from the ignition, the bulky key ring jingling in his hand. The throaty rumble of his five-year-old Mustang cuts off, plunging us into silence. "Are you *sure* you want to do this?"

I fight the urge to smile and instead slide deeper into the smooth bucket seat, trying not to fidget. I smooth out my sequined teal miniskirt and peer into the darkness, trying to make out some of the shadowy figures approaching Carter's house.

Carter Wellesley is Mossy Rock High School's golden boy, the one with the flawless smile and wicked fastball. He's captain of the football, basketball, and baseball teams. I guess that's not a huge accomplishment, considering that anyone with the slightest athletic ability is practically drafted onto the team, but he makes it look effortless. He's not brilliant, but he's funny, and people are drawn to him like a moth to flame. And aside from dating Tracey for a record-breaking two months, he's not into attachment, at least as far as I can tell.

In the twelve years we've gone to school together, I've watched him flirt with every girl—including me, once, although he might have been joking with the girl next to me. Most guys do ignore me, after all. But he's still a flirt, which is why he's the perfect one for tonight.

It's barely nine, but the bash is quickly reaching full steam. Even from our curbside vantage point, I can tell that most of the school is already here. Not that it means much—our senior class has forty-seven students. Forty-five, if you nix the stoner twins who have hardly shown up at all this month.

"Yes, I'm sure," I say with fake confidence, the cheap sequins digging into my palms. I force myself to let go of the skirt before I ruin it. "We graduate in a week. If I don't do it now, Carter will never even know my name."

"He knows your name. You've known him since kindergarten. It's impossible to *not* know your name."

I shoot Nick a glare. "Sometimes he calls me Pam."

"He probably does that on purpose. Besides, at least it *rhymes* with Sam."

I narrow my eyes further. "Don't be stupid, Nick."

"*Don't be stupid, Nick*," he parrots back at me, in an annoying, nasally voice. There's no way I sound like that. He's pissed off, and I let myself hope that means something. Why else would he get riled up about me going after Carter? God let me be right.

Nick blows out a long, slow breath and leans his head against the headrest again, which will probably make his bed-head look even more attractive to the girls at the party. The messier his thick brown hair gets, the more they cling to him like Reynolds Wrap. I bet if he used his graphing calculator, he could show the exact moment that he would get the maximum effect.

Must be nice. I spent forty-five minutes tonight trying to tame my dark blond curls into something resembling Taylor Swift, but I look more like a Lady Gaga–inspired disaster. Nothing new, though. No matter what I do, average is the best I can hope for. That's all I want. Average. Cute if I'm lucky. I'll probably always fall short of downright pretty.

I'm struck again by the dull pain of thinking that maybe if my mom were still around, she could help me.

Could show me how to dress better, how to use the right makeup to obscure my too-big nose, fix my too-small eyes.

I stare Nick down, but now he won't look at me. I think I have a heart arrhythmia now—it's spasming, all thud *thud* thud *thud*.

He's mad I'm interested in Carter. He's upset I'm dressed in a miniskirt. He won't meet my eyes. Please let this mean what I think it means.

"Your dad would kill both of us if he saw you in that," he says, resignation in his voice.

"Which is why he'll never know."

"You know this is a bad idea," he adds, staring out the windshield.

"No, it is *not* a bad idea. Carter broke up with Tracey two weeks ago. The timing is perfect." Why is Nick so intent on talking me out of it? Is it because he thinks I'm not pretty enough for Carter, or because he actually likes me?

I grip the door handle. "Seriously," I say, "stop trying to psych me out. I'm doing it."

"Whatever," he says gruffly. " Let's just go in."

I nod, try not to visibly gulp. I climb out of the car and slam the door extra hard, ignoring the wince Nick gives me. I grip my purse in one hand and use the other to adjust the miniskirt that seems to have ridden up so high I might be showing off my thong.

Thong. I can't believe I bought one of those ridiculous things. But I've watched Carter for four years, and he doesn't go for my usual look: T-shirts and Levis. Carter is high school perfection—a man's man who actually has manners, a guy who can fix a car but also knows to open doors and buy flowers for his girlfriend. Well, before they broke up.

I chose him because it's the obvious choice. He's single, and he's flirty, and that's all I need.

I take in a long breath and blow it out through my mouth as I stride across a lawn so well-manicured it would make a golf course proud, Nick trailing behind. My shiny-new stilettos sort of sink into the grass, so I move over to the walkway.

There are three guys sitting on a brick planter to my right, and I can feel their eyes boring right into me. The confidence I faked in the car disappears completely and I try to walk as if I don't notice them watching me.

I totter my way to the front door, following a lanky redhead in a spaghetti-strap tank top and jeans so tight they look painted on. When the leaded-glass and oak door swings open, a bass beat rumbles out. It sounds like Flo Rida. Figures Carter would listen to this stuff. What's wrong with a little country?

The crowd inside is thick. I have to turn sideways to squeeze in far enough to let Nick enter behind me. Even with its cavernous, twenty-foot ceilings, the house feels a little cramped.

I get caught in a stream of people—jammed in the mix, shoulder-to-shoulder—and it forces me to migrate away from Nick, toward the kitchen. I don't know where

Carter even found this many people. Maybe there are juniors here, too.

I know I'm too smashed-in for people to notice me or what I'm wearing, but I feel like every eye in the room is on me. It's warm, and it feels as if every inch of my skin is already glistening with sweat. This was a bad idea. What had sounded brilliant in the safe cocoon of my bedroom now seems ridiculous.

But if I stick with it, I know it'll work. Nick will see me flirt, and he'll feel that same twinge I did the first time I saw him with Reyna—a dull ache that takes up residence in your chest.

A long plastic trough filled with ice and bottles of alcohol is all the invitation I need. I grab the first thing I see—hard lemonade—and twist off the cap. I take a long, relentless drink, downing at least half of it in one swoop. I'm not a drinker, not normally. My dad's a cop—the chief of police, in fact—and he'd kill me if he knew I went out partying like this. As it is, he thinks I'm at a mock U.N. meeting. I don't even think we have those at our school, but he doesn't actually know anything about me or who I am, so he didn't think much of it.

I've only been drunk once, sophomore year, when Nick and I were sneaking alcohol out of the cooler during a particularly busy Fourth of July barbecue at his house. But right now the butterflies are multiplying too fast. I just need this one drink. Maybe two. Then I can reassess the plan. Possibly ditch it all together.

The effect of the alcohol is almost instant. It's like

warm fingers unfurling inside my stomach. I guzzle the rest of the bottle, then toss it and pick up a beer, relishing the quieting of the butterflies.

I sip the beer, finally turning away from the granite counter and looking back into the great room. Finals are mostly over and it seems like the entire senior class is here to celebrate. I guess that's nothing crazy, in a town this small. This stifling. What else is there to do?

Scanning the crowd, I look for Carter's perfect, shaggy blond hair and intense blue eyes. It's too warm in here for his trademark letterman jacket—the one positively filled with patches representing every sport he's mastered.

Instead, my eyes land on Nick. He's still stuck near the door, and already people are gravitating toward him, high-fiving him and slapping his back, trading jokes and barbs. You'd think he just won an Oscar for Best Motion Picture or something, the way everyone carries on. He's the class president, not a celebrity.

He meets my eyes, nodding, and I tip my chin up back at him. And then the moment scatters, as a tall brunette with exotic dark eyes flings her arms around him.

It's Reyna, the ex-girlfriend. No—wait—girlfriend, without the ex attached. I think. She looks a little drunk, what with the awkward sloppiness of the hug.

Oh God, we're wearing the same obnoxious sequined miniskirt. But she was smart enough to wear it with low gladiator sandals instead of sky-high stilettos. She looks beach chic; I look like a go-go dancer. I knew I went overboard.

I tear my eyes away from them, feeling my cheeks flame, and guzzle the beer in my hand until it's empty. The heat I now feel is not due to embarrassment.

The energy in the room seems to hum and change, and I realize that Carter has walked in. Maybe "walk" is the wrong word. He seems to glide, floating into the room as if he's above everyone else, as if he doesn't need to touch the ground like us mere mortals. And people part like the Red Sea for him, smiling, waving, staring. I'm surprised they don't drop to their knees and bow.

He's walking toward me. *Straight* toward me. I try to breathe in slowly, keep the pressure from squeezing my lungs too tightly. I need this to work. I need him to notice me, flirt with me, laugh with me. Nick is just across the room. If he saw Carter sling an arm around me, saw him tuck a tendril of hair behind my ear, maybe, finally, Nick would do something. Swoop in and admit he has feelings for me. Because no matter how hard I try, I can't make the first move. Can't just *ask* him.

It's stupid and I know that, but if I ask him and don't like what he says, it'll kill me. And it'll kill our friendship. I just can't take it if his answer isn't yes.

When Carter meets my eyes, gives me that glowing smile of his, I'm like butter in a hot pan. I think I might melt right into my terribly uncomfortable shoes. He's dazzling—it's no wonder all the girls are after him.

"Hey," he says, stopping so near me that our toes seem to touch. His presence is more intense than ever. I want to shrink back and lean forward at the same time. I never realized how tall he is—almost as tall as Nick. He must be six foot. And I'm five three on a good day.

"Hi," I say in my perkiest voice, smiling so widely he can probably tell I've had my wisdom teeth pulled.

Way to look crazy. I probably should have stuck with that flippant, bored look that his ex, Tracey, has mastered. Does he like it if girls come on strong? It's not like I'm going to sleep with him, of course. I'd never go that far. I just need to flirt with him, maybe get him to give me a playful pinch, tug on one of my curls, *something*.

We share a long, silent moment. I smile demurely in his direction. I think. I'm not entirely sure what smiling demurely feels like. I try to find something intelligent to say. Something to break the ice, get us talking. Something flirty that will let him know I'm interested.

Then he clears his throat and raises his eyebrows. My smile falters. I can't read his look.

"Um, you're blocking the beer," he says. His voice is booming. *So loud.*

I think I hear someone snicker.

"What?" Every move I make is weird, jerky, mechanical. I have lost all ability to control myself. My heart lands somewhere in my feet. I'm making a fool of myself. This will never work.

I twist around and realize I've been standing in front of the beer trough. And since there are so many people gathered around, Carter can't get to it.

"Uh . . . oh."

I step back, knocking right into someone else, and

Carter reaches forward. He grabs two bottles by the neck and then steps away from me.

"Thanks," he says, and for one millisecond he meets my eyes and I feel the glow of his look, realize what it would feel like if he cared who I was, if I was one of the pretty girls. I truly get why other girls are enamored of him, why they'd do anything to catch his eye.

But I can't say "you're welcome" before he's already gone, vanished into the crowd. This isn't how I imagined it. It's not how it would work in one of my books.

I pop the top off a beer and take another long, lonely drink.

———

I've lost Nick. He vanished at least an hour ago. And he's my ride home.

I picture him flirting with Reyna, and it stings. And that's why I haven't moved, haven't gone to look for him. Because I don't need to see it, don't need to confirm it. The crowd has thinned out some and we're quickly approaching midnight. If I don't get home soon, my dad will know the model U.N. excuse was a complete fabrication. There aren't any schools we would compete against that are more than an hour and a half away.

I'm thoroughly drunk. Not "I'm going to puke right on my own high heels" drunk, but "dancing on a couch sounds like a really good idea" drunk.

Ever since the epic fail with Carter, I've been sitting

on a stool in the kitchen, sipping beer. Even though I've known all these people my entire life, no one really seems to care if they know me. Sure, they know who I am. We all know each other. I share at least two classes with every one of them. But picking me out of a lineup and knowing who I *really* am? Two different things. A year from now, when they're all in college in some far-flung state, if someone asked them my name, they'd probably squint, tip their head, and vaguely remember me as that blonde who sat behind them in math. Who they were paired with in gym.

I wish I'd worn my jeans, because the stool is sticking to my thighs and I can't stop tugging at my too-short hemline. People keep glancing my way, as if shocked I'm wearing something other than jeans, and I want to snap at them to take a picture because it would last longer. But I don't.

There are four bottles sitting next to me. Four *empty* bottles. Everything is so warm and fuzzy, I can barely muster annoyance at Carter any more.

I guess I knew this wouldn't work. That I didn't have a chance at getting Carter's attention. I just thought if I dressed the part, he'd notice me, react to me enough to catch Nick's attention.

But Nick probably knew all along that Carter would blow me off.

I sigh and take another sip of the now-empty bottle. Maybe I didn't come on strong enough. Maybe I should give it another shot. Go find him, flirt with him, make sure Nick sees us. That's all I need. Maybe there's a way to do it where Carter's participation is limited. I can just laugh like he said something outrageously funny. Touch his knee or slug him in the arm or something.

I get up, wobbling more than ever on the tall heels, and make my way down the hall. I'm pretty sure there's a game room somewhere down here, as I've heard people talking about a pool table. The hall seems like it's tilting just a little bit as I cross the space. It's like walking across the deck of a boat.

Just as I round a corner, I see Carter. Tall, muscular, perfect, in that long-sleeved cotton tee that barely stretches across the muscles he's built during four years of nonstop sports. Normally, guys like Carter stay here in town after graduation, waste away forever. Have two kids, find work at the lumber mill in Morton. Buy a house when they turn twenty and stay put forever.

I wonder what his plans are.

He slips into a bedroom, and my heart thumps even harder. I wonder if it's his. But I need him to go back to the party, where Nick and everyone else is.

My feet seem to propel me forward of their own accord, following Carter as if magnetized. Somewhere along the way the hallway wall looms closer, and I have to put my hand out to keep from knocking right into it. Maybe I'm a little more drunk than I thought. I take in a deep breath to steady myself, then continue on.

I stop briefly at the door, which he's left open a few inches. My hand shakes as I reach out and rest my palm flat against the painted, six-panel slab. I nudge it open. It's nearly dark inside; a small lamp on the desk in one corner illuminates the space enough that I can see shadows. Carter's broad back is to me, and he's rifling through a drawer in his dresser.

I step further into the room and look around. It looks exactly as I'd expected it to: masculine, filled with dark woods and rumpled, navy blue sheets, sports memorabilia adorning the beige walls. A big Seahawks pennant hangs over his bed. I close my eyes and breathe deeply just to see how it smells. Fresh. Like laundry or Pine-Sol, but something spicy, too, like aftershave. Carter has a smooth, clean-cut jaw. Does he have to shave every morning?

My heels sink in the thick carpeting, and my eyes pop open as I wobble, putting a hand out to save myself. It lands on the door and slams it shut.

Carter whirls around, spooked.

"Oh, sorry," I say. I clear my throat. My heart is galloping so hard in my chest it might break free and leave the room entirely. "I, uh, lost my balance."

"What are you doing?" His words are so loud they seem to fill the room up.

I take in a long, slow breath. "I wanted to talk to you."

"So talk," he says. His voice isn't harsh, but it's not all that inviting either. In the darkness of the room, shadows fill his face and it's hard to make out his expression.

I run a hand through my hair, and it tangles in my curls. "I just…" I step forward, the heels still sinking terribly in the plush carpet. The space between us diminishes until I'm so close I could touch him.

I take the last step, but my heel lands on something uneven, something I hadn't seen in the dark. My ankle turns and my arms fly upward, and Carter reaches forward, but his dresser is closer. I hit my cheek on the edge of it and my body twists, and one of the knobs on the middle drawer catches the delicate lace strap on my tank top.

It rips as I hit the floor. My face could burst into flames at any moment. I probably should not have had that fourth beer. Or was it the fifth? There was that hard lemonade...

I feel myself being pulled upward, feel Carter's strong hands under my arms. I teeter in front of him, staring upward at his intense, dark eyes. "Thank you," I say. He hasn't let go of me. My cheek pulses as his hands slide off of me, and I sway for a half a second until I regain my balance.

"What are you doing in here?"

"What?" my voice sounds ridiculous, high-pitched and squeaky. Why am I so nervous? It's not like I actually want to throw myself at him. "Uh, I don't know. I just thought..." My voice trails off. I hadn't actually planned in advance *how* to get him back out to the party. "I just thought..."

"Thought what? You thought *I'd* want *you*?"

I blink, my eyes finally adjusting to the darkness enough that I can see him. See his sneer and the cold, disgusted look in his slightly glazed eyes. He's drunk, like me, and his look of pure disgust isn't even a little guarded.

Carter has never looked so ugly.

"Are you kidding me?" he asks.

My jaw drops. It's like my tongue is swollen, blocking me from talking. I swallow two, three times, the pain growing. Of course he doesn't want me. "No. Not at all. I just—"

"Look, your body isn't bad," he says, scanning me, pausing at the place where my skirt barely covers six inches of my thighs. "Nice legs, and all. But you're like … a two-bagger. Get real."

A tear runs down my cheek before I even feel my eyes moisten, my heart twisting in a vice as new heat blooms on my cheeks. Even drunk, I know what he's saying. Once, at a football game, I heard two guys talk about how a girl was so ugly, if they wanted to sleep with her they'd have to put a bag over her head, and one over theirs, too, just in case her bag fell off.

She was a *two-bagger*.

I swallow a gag.

The room spins harder. I reach up to slap him but he's faster, and grabs my wrist. He shakes his head, slowly, staring me straight in the eyes with a mocking look. It's like he loves that I tried to hit him. My murky brain can't seem to process that.

Then he steps back, away from me, and heads for the door.

I follow him. I want to scream, leap on his back, rip out his hair. I want to tell him what I was doing, make him understand that I don't even want him like he thinks I do, but that would make me seem insane.

I want to do something…anything…to make him understand he just shattered me, spoke the very things I always hear in my head, the things I *know* Nick thinks about me. The reason I'm stuck firmly in friend territory. But I can't get my legs to move any faster, and he's leaving the room before I've figured it out.

I'm only a few steps behind him, and I'm out in the hall before I realize I've made a mistake. I should have composed myself first. My eyes are filled with tears, shimmering, making everything dance. I rush to fix my top, but there's nothing I can do. The strap just kind of hangs there, exposing the edge of my bra.

"Oh my God, are you okay?"

I look up to realize I'm standing directly in front of Michelle Pattison. We did a project together once. I can't remember what it was. Her jaw is hanging loose, like it's completely unhinged.

I blink rapidly, trying to clear my eyes. My cheek is pounding now, and I wince when Michelle reaches out like she's going to touch it. I step back.

"Carter Wellesley is a complete, total asshole," I say. My voice is wobbly and gargled. My lip starts to tremble as the hurt prevails over my attempt at composure. "I can't *believe* him. He…he…"

A dark look passes over Michelle's refined ivory features. Her eyes sweep over me and then she looks over her shoulder, in the direction Carter went. "Did he…I mean, did he just…"

I nod my head, though I'm not really listening to her.

Her words just float around me, land somewhere at my feet. I think she's still talking. More tears slide loose and I nod again and then stumble past her, shoving her out of my way as I stagger down the hall.

I have to get out of here before I totally fall apart.

I knock into a couple making out and trip over their feet, which sends me careening into a closed door. I hit it so hard the sound seems to echo everywhere, even over the loud music.

Everyone is staring.

I rush toward the foyer, yank open the door, and walk out into the night.

I don't care if I have to walk all three miles home.

Two

I burrow my head deeper into my pillow, ignoring the yellow beam of light warming my face. How can it be morning already? I can't possibly get up while my head pounds this hard. Without opening my eyes, I reach out to find the quilt and throw it over my head.

I twist around, trying to find a comfortable way to lie that doesn't make it feel like the black on the back of my eye lids is spinning. But it doesn't work, and my bed feels like I'm bobbing on the ocean current. I sit up quickly, nausea burning my throat. I rush to my little bathroom, tripping over my discarded stilettos and landing on my knees just in time to vomit the meager contents of my stomach into the toilet.

I will never drink again. Never, *ever* again. My dad was right to tell me I shouldn't do it. His rules usually have purposes, and this is one of them.

I grip the porcelain as I heave one more time, then flush the toilet and rock back on my heels, wiping my mouth with toilet paper. The bathroom swims into focus as I lean against the wall, the heater vent beside me kicking on and blowing my hair around.

My heels lie next to me on the linoleum, caked with mud. I narrow my eyes. How did I get mud all over my shoes?

I blink, some fuzzy memory swimming to the surface. The ball fields at the elementary school down the street. I cut through them on my way home, my heels sinking into the dirt and making it impossible to walk in a straight line. I was halfway across when I pulled the shoes off and walked barefoot the rest of the way, my fingers hooked around the straps.

I try to remember why I walked home, but my mind is spinning so hard it's impossible to think. I groan and rub my face with my hands, but I jerk one hand away when my cheek throbs. I gently probe the skin with my fingertips, wincing.

I use the towel bar to stagger to my feet and go to the mirror. The reflection staring back at me is mine, and yet there's an angry red mark on my cheek that doesn't belong there. I blink, willing the pounding to cease long enough for me to focus.

The last thing I remember is … sitting in the kitchen at Carter's house. Drinking. Stupid drinking! Why did I think that was a good idea?

No … I remember following him. Somewhere. A room. *His* room.

His dresser. I fell down. Right in front of him, like a total idiotic klutz, I fell down.

I blink several times to clear my fuzzy brain, but it doesn't help. I had no idea hangovers could feel like this. The other time I drank, with Nick, we only dared sneak a few bottles. I must have had five or six last night. Maybe more, because it's all pretty fuzzy. That's probably a lot of beer for someone who weighs a puny hundred pounds.

I sink back to the floor and end up lying down, my non-injured cheek smashed to the cool linoleum. I mopped this floor yesterday, so I know it's clean. And right now I don't even care. I cover myself with a towel and close my eyes, hoping all of this just … goes away.

Two-bagger. He called me a two-bagger. I bury my face in my hands and groan.

The house is gloriously silent; my dad is on the grave-yard shift, and then he'll go back to the station to organize his paperwork … then go by the coffee shop … he won't be around for a few hours to harp on me about chores or homework or … hangovers. Horrible, horrible hangovers.

I struggle to my feet and pull out my toothbrush,

slathering it liberally with toothpaste before shoving it into my mouth and scrubbing for all I'm worth.

I pause to spit out the foam in my mouth and then switch to scrubbing on the other side and stare at my reflection in the mirror. I look like death warmed over, with a bright red splotch on one cheek and mascara tracks down both my cheeks.

I turn and flip on the shower, twisting the handle to put it on as strong and as hot as it gets.

It takes me thirty minutes, gallons of scalding water, and about seventeen makeup products, but eventually I look good as new. The pinkish hue of the bruise has been obscured, and the mascara tracks are scrubbed clean.

I don't *feel* good as new, but whatever. Fake it 'til ya make it.

Or something.

I go to my room and drop to my knees, pulling out the pile of notebooks under my bed. My failed attempts at writing books as good as the ones I read. I've never finished any of them, and I've definitely never shown them to anyone.

Six, seven, eight of them. Filled with my loopy scrawl. Filled with romantic stories. I'm a cheerleader in one, a damsel in distress in another, a secret agent in the third. The only thing that's constant is that Nick shows up every time and saves the day, then professes his love to me and we walk off into the proverbial sunset. No one knows about these stories, least of all Nick. He knows I want to study English in college, but he doesn't know about the creative writing part.

I open the first notebook and rip. The first page, the second, the third. I shred everything out of it until there's a huge pile of crumpled, mangled paper in front of me.

I'm angry. Totally pissed off. Not only will Nick never want me, but Carter laughed at the mere *idea* of wanting me. Is it possible to be a bigger loser than I am? Probably not. It takes twenty minutes to shred every notebook and throw it all in the trash, then drag the bag out and toss it into the can at the curb.

I'll write something new. Something that actually resembles reality; I can't pine over Nick for the rest of my life. Maybe I'll be the crazy cat lady by the end of the story, but at least it would be real. How did I ever think Nick could want me? Carter sure didn't.

Minutes later I'm curled up in my computer chair, playing an online puzzle game that barely manages to keep my brain from wandering to last night, when Nick flings my bedroom door open without bothering to knock. "'Mornin', sunshine!"

I try not to wince at his loud, perky voice. Instead, I stare at my computer screen. "I'm not talking to you."

He furrows his brow. "Why?"

"You let me walk home. By myself," I say. Hello, did he not even notice I wasn't in his car? Thank God the bruise is covered up now; I don't even want to explain that one to him.

"I did not. You left without saying goodbye. I was in

the billiards room the whole time." He pauses in the doorway. "Your dad going to be home any time soon?

"No, not 'til at least one or two." I spin around in my rolly chair, doing my best to glare at him. "And what were you doing in the billiards room all night? Killing Professor Plum with a candlestick?"

Nick flings himself onto my bed. "Of course not. It was the lead pipe. Do I look like a guy who walks around with a candlestick?"

I turn back to my desk and flip the laptop screen down, then give him another pointed look. "As if you walk around with a lead pipe, either. Though I suppose I'd buy that you were off in some corner with Little Miss Scarlett."

The jealousy creeps into my voice and I hate myself a little more. How has he not figured me out yet? I'm not even doing a very good job at hiding it these days, which only makes me feel more pathetic. Truth is, it's impossible to hide it. Every time I'm near him, I just want to hug him. Touch him. Say the words that seem forever lodged in my throat. But all I ever do is stand there.

I want him to know. But then again I don't.

"What? I looked everywhere when I was ready to go, but you were already gone. I asked every one there, and Michelle Pattison said she saw you leaving. How is it my fault you walked home?"

Michelle Pattison. Oh God, she saw me leave in tears. This is not good. Michelle has this goody-two-shoes persona, but she's a terrible gossip. My stomach clenches again. I don't want people to know what happened in

Carter's room. Did I close the door when I walked in? Or did she hear the whole thing? I wonder if she laughed. I wonder if she thought I went in there to throw myself at him.

I wonder if Nick heard anything. He must not have, or why would he be acting so normal right now?

"Oh, whatever," I say. "Obviously you were too into Scarlett to care what I was up to." There it is again, that little edge to my voice.

"How'd things go with Carter?" Nick says, in an obvious attempt to change the topic.

I sigh, my ugly curly bangs fluffing in the breeze of it. Obviously Nick didn't hear about my moment of glory. Seems I really am a two-bagger. That's why guys never ask me out, why Nick is happy to be friends with me and doesn't see me any other way.

"Okay," I lie. "We were in his room for a while."

Nick gives me a sharp look, and I nearly blurt out the truth. "You were?"

"Uh-huh." I pick at my toenails and hope he doesn't ask any more questions. I can bluff for about thirty seconds, but I don't think I can keep this up if he pushes it.

He rolls over onto his back and laces his fingers behind his head, staring upward at the glow-in-the-dark stars we applied five years ago. I remember how we rolled my bed around the room and then stood on it and spent all afternoon jumping up and down, placing stars all over the place. Half of them have already fallen off. Just like most things in my life. Halfway between perfect and a total failure.

"Do you want to go to Olympia?" he asks, still staring at the ceiling.

I grin. He actually *is* irritated at the idea that I was with Carter in his room. Maybe it isn't hopeless. Maybe, for one millisecond, he pictured me with Carter and didn't like it.

"No thanks," I say. "I'd rather wear a miniskirt."

"You did—last night." I can almost *hear* his sly smile. He's mocking me. I probably looked just as comfortable in that thing as I felt.

"That was a one-time occurrence. It'll be going in the trash can later today." I want to throw something at him. I eyeball the big plastic stapler on my desk. It's holding down a magazine, under which I've hidden my acceptance paperwork for University of Washington. It's not just a few sheets of paper. It's my key to freedom.

"Good, because it's kind of irritating."

I narrow my eyes. Before he said that, I'd never wanted to wear another miniskirt. But now I want to put one on just to spite him. "What the hell?" I snap. "Just don't look at me, then."

"I didn't. But jeez, everyone else did."

My lips twitch. Maybe I hadn't needed Carter after all. Maybe I just needed a mini and heels. Maybe there's a reason the popular crowd dresses like that. I kind of like the idea of guys checking me out.

"Really?" I ask.

"Right, like you didn't notice." He picks his head up

just enough to see the pleased grin that must be lighting up my face.

"Who was looking?"

"I am *not* going there with you."

"Whatever, Saint Nick," I say, grinning even wider. Was Nick checking me out? Is that even possible?

"I hate it when you call me that." He picks up the small pillow next to his head and lobs it at me without looking. I snag it out of the air and throw it back before he can react, and it nails him in the face. He grins, and I know *it's on*. He grabs all three pillows off my bed and I shriek and dive to the floor, but they still hit me, falling around me like atomic bombs.

As soon as it stops, I leap to my feet and launch myself at him, and somehow I end up straddling him with a pillow in each hand. He grins and tries to block his face, but I bombard him from both sides. Before I know what's happening, he bucks violently and I end up twisted, under him. His eyes are sparkling, the brightest shade of blue I've ever seen them. Brilliant, like the spring skyline on a cloudless day.

"You're such an ass," I say. Egging Nick on is the best part of my life. The best part of our relationship. There aren't many things I'm good at, but with Nick, I always win. It's why I can't stop wanting to be around him, why I can't stop dreaming there could be something beyond *this*. This dancing around it, this best-friends-who-wrestle, this tension I'm afraid that only I feel.

Why does it have to be so damned complicated?

And why *isn't* it complicated to him?

He rolls his eyes, but for one long, lingering moment he continues to hover there, not saying anything, not moving, not *anything*. I swallow, my breathing turned shallow.

The moment stretches on long enough to make me suddenly aware of the way our chests are heaving, the intensity in his stare, the way one of his legs is lying against mine in a way that makes our thighs touch.

He furrows his brow and leans in. "Why are you wearing so much makeup?"

So you won't see my bruise. Instead of saying it, though, I shove him off of me. "Why, do I look like a clown or something?"

I climb to my feet, reining my breathing in as I go to the bathroom and flip on the light, leaning in to peer at my reflection. I don't look *that* bad, do I? I mean, I don't normally wear this much, but I so don't want to explain the bruise to Nick or anyone else.

He steps up behind me, watches me survey myself in the mirror. "No, you look really good." His voice lowers. "Actually ... pretty."

My mouth goes dry. What does that mean? "Actually pretty" like ... for once I actually look pretty? Or, "Actually, you look really pretty." I want to ask, but that would be pathetic. Fishing for compliments.

Nick has never called me pretty. So I roll my eyes and flip the light off. "And you obviously need to get laid," I say, leaving the bathroom.

He follows me out to my room. "I did. Last night."

My heart plunges into my stomach and it takes everything I have to give him a flippant look. "Ewww, don't want to know!" I plug my ears and start humming a tune, as if the mere idea of hearing it is too disgusting to deal with. If only he knew.

He gets a devilish gleam to his eyes and I unplug my ears. "Are you sure? Because she was … "

I plug my ears again, my heart jammed into my throat. "*No!* Seriously, go tell your guy friends. TMI, Nick, TMI."

Sometimes I just *don't* want to be one of the guys. Well, most of the time.

All of the time.

He shrugs. "Hey, you asked."

I pull my fingers out of my ears. "Whatever. Do you want to play the Wii or what?"

"Obviously."

We leave my bedroom, heading to the den downstairs. My grandma gave me this thing for Christmas last year, and Nick and I have racked up countless hours playing it.

I toss a remote to Nick, and he bumbles and drops it. Nick has the athletic ability of a giraffe, all flying limbs and bad coordination. Thank God for that because otherwise I'd be convinced he's some kind of teenage cyborg. Knowing he has one thing he's terrible at is what makes it possible to not hate him for being so perfect.

"So, who did you hook up with?" I ask, navigating the curser on the screen until it selects a ridiculous Mii that has perfect blond hair, wide blue eyes, and pretty, perfect eyebrows. She's the me I'd be if I knew my way around a makeup counter.

"I thought it was TMI," he says, raising a brow.

"Was it Reyna?"

"Yeah." Nick clicks on the dark-haired Mii that he created the day we unpacked the console. He has at least six different avatars to choose from. Sometimes we spend hours playing this stupid tennis game. Yale-bound Nick probably needs as much mindless activity as I do.

I cross my arms. "So you're not broken up."

"On a break."

"A break that includes sleeping together?" I give him a look and then go back to the screen and select the tennis game, pretending like we're talking about the weather and not something that wrenches my gut.

The court rolls on screen.

"We're friends with benefits." Nick seems awfully busy adjusting the wrist strap on his controller. I want to study him but instead I pretend to be concentrating on position-ing my fingers over the buttons.

"I think she's getting robbed in the benefits depart-ment." I grin, masking my pain, and then slam the remote down and the ball sails past Nick before he can move.

He pretends to be outraged by my maneuver, his eyebrows raised in a mock-look of haughtiness. "You're just jealous."

"Of what? I get to be friends with you and I don't have to give it up." I try to fake a laugh and seem to choke on it.

"Plenty of women would *pay* for this." He slams the

ball back to me and I jump to the side in time to send it skittering across the top of the net. We volley the digital ball back and forth a few times in silence.

My phone beeps, so I pull it out of my pocket. A text message. The only person who ever texts me is Nick, and I'm standing right next to him. I click on the envelope icon.

> Hey, just wanted to make sure ur ok—u looked super upset last nite. Let me know if u need anything. X, Michelle.

Huh? How did she even get my phone number?

I read the text again. Why does she even care? We're not friends or anything.

"What's up?" Nick asks, glancing down at my phone.

"Huh? Oh. Nothing." I shove the phone back into my pocket.

Nick gives me a lingering look, but doesn't push it. "So, are you nervous?"

"About?"

"School." He shrugs.

I miss the ball and scowl. Nick's limbs fly around as he tries to serve and misses. "What, like finals?" I ask. "All I have left is Chemistry."

He shakes his head. "No, college."

"Oh." I chew on my lip, picturing myself at UW, walking the rolling hills as the crimson leaves fall from nearby trees. In the distance, the sparkling water of Lake Washington beckons. For the first time, my dad isn't seconds away. He won't round the corner and send my heart slamming into my throat. He won't lecture me every night about grades, about clothes, about everything.

He won't anything. It'll be the first time in my life he won't be breathing down my neck. I wonder if I'll finally figure out who I am, forge some kind of identity that doesn't forever skate under the radar.

It's always a melancholy picture, though, because I'm totally alone and Nick is on the other side of the country. I'll finally know what it's like without him buffering me from the extreme silence of having no friends, no allies, no one.

"Not really," I say. "I mean, it'll just be general education requirements at first. English, math, that kind of stuff."

"I didn't mean the courses. Why is it always the academics you think of first?"

I snort. "Uh, because that's sort of the point of going to college?"

He shrugs. "There's more to it, though. There's a reason everyone calls it *the college experience*." There's a little bit of an edge to his voice.

I turn and furrow my brows, giving him a long look. I *am* freaked out about the social aspect, but I'll never tell Nick that. And he's the guy who can charm the parka off an Eskimo, so what's he concerned about?

"Nicholas Davis, are you nervous you won't make any frieeeeennnnnnnds?" I say, stretching the word out so it sounds all singsong, unable to contain my grin. Nick is never nervous.

He glares at me and I realize I've struck a chord.

"Oh stop giving me that look. You're just worried because you're all *big fish in a small pond* now, but give me a break. When it comes to college, you'll have no problem. I give you forty-two minutes on campus before someone has signed up to replace me."

He gives me a sharp look. "No one is replacing you."

I shrug. "Not like I'm going to be around to fill the position."

"Sam, we're best friends. That's not going to change just because a few miles separate us."

"Try a few thousand."

"Still. We'll be home for Thanksgiving and Christmas and all summer long. And you can come out east for spring break."

I look down at my remote. Sorrow swirls through me. I'm not as smart as Nick. He knew when he applied to the ivies that I wouldn't be going there. I can't blame him, but the hurt won't go away, either. Sometimes I think about telling him I'll go to some silly community college on the East Coast just to be with him. We'll get a two-bedroom apartment, and the two-dozen yards currently between our bedrooms will become about two feet, and we won't have to part ways at all. And maybe, eventually, we won't need two bedrooms.

But every time I want to tell him this, I just get choked up.

I know the truth: in a couple of months, he's going to walk out of my life and forget to glance back. It's why I feel a little more panicky every day. I never pictured my life without him in it, and suddenly it's all I can see, and he doesn't seem as freaked out by this as I am.

He gives up on playing, letting the remote dangle from his wrist. The spectators on screen bob up and down, cheering over the missed ball. "Why are we even talking about this stuff? I thought we were playing Wii."

"We were. We can talk and play," I say. "Well, I can. You, not so much."

"Give a guy a little credit, would you?" He has the audacity to act hurt. As if his ego needs massaging.

I smirk. How is it so easy for him to turn things around? "Get real. You know your brother soaked up all the athletic genes in your gene pool."

"You wound me. You really do." Nick puts a hand to his heart.

I roll my eyes and queue up the game again. "Would you like a Band-Aid? A sippy cup, maybe?"

He sighs, a big dramatic sigh that could win him an Oscar. "Okay, okay, it's on. You're going down this time."

"A sloth could beat you at this game. The sooner you come to terms with this, the sooner we can move on."

"Never!" He hits the start button and whacks the imaginary ball, hard, and it sails so fast I leap back and thrash at the same time, barely managing to whack it back. It streaks across the net and right past Nick's Mii, which is failing spectacularly at catching it.

"You were saying?"

His eyes shimmer in that happy, glowing way of his. The way that lights up my dreams. "I'm going to miss you this fall," he says.

"Yeah. Me too. I'm really going to miss me."

"Shut up." He's smiling at me.

I try to look unimpressed. "You're such a dork."

"That's why you love me," he says, whacking the ball.

His last words ring over and over again, because sometimes I really wonder if he knows.

Three

On Sunday, I climb into Nick's car as hard rock blasts from the speakers. He reaches to turn it down, waiting quietly while I buckle my seat belt before shifting into reverse and gliding out of the driveway. For a moment as he pulls away, the throaty rumble of his car competes with the radio, and we glide down the fir-tree-lined streets without speaking.

"Are you so totally stoked?" he asks, signaling right and heading toward the main drag.

I snort. "I just keep reminding myself this is the last time we have to do this."

Nick glances over at me as he comes to a stop at the

blinking red light. "Aren't you the one that talked *me* into this?"

"Yeah. Three months ago. When I thought we'd be walking dogs, not washing them. And before I got sick of driving all the way to Chehalis just to wash said dogs."

Our town, Mossyrock, is over twenty miles away from real freeways, tucked up against the evergreen-filled Cascade Mountain range and Riffe Lake, an enormous, sparkling, man-made lake. The closest humane society is in Chehalis, near I-5. It's a full half-hour drive.

"Now, now, where's that speech about the greater good of the world?"

I blow out an irritated sigh. "Must you be so high and mighty this early in the morning?"

Nick taps on the radio. "It's nine thirty."

"On a Sunday."

He shrugs. "Still nine thirty."

"I am so signing up for night classes at UW."

Nick turns onto Jarvis road and I realize we're going to pass right by Carter's house. I sink further into the seat. I don't want to even *think* about what happened in Carter's room.

"Jesus, look at Carter's car." Nick points as he slows his Mustang. We glide past the black Charger sitting at the curb in front of Carter's house.

Yellow egg yolks have left streaks down the glossy black paint.

"Wow, that…sucks." I sit up, stare at the car. I'd think someone was excluded from the guest list, but that's stupid. Heck, I was there. This is Mossyrock—everyone's invited everywhere. You can't have a party *and* be exclusive in this town.

I can't help but feel just a little bit smug as I think of Carter insulting me. Maybe he sorta deserves the eggs.

Nick nods. "I'll text him when we get to the humane society. He's not gonna want to let that sit."

I nod, but I secretly hope Nick forgets.

———————

Nick pulls into the parking lot at the humane society. I reluctantly unbuckle as he digs out his phone, fires off a text message, then drops it back into the center console.

When we reach the entry, Nick holds the door open and I slip past him.

"Hey guys," the receptionist calls. She's wearing scrubs with bright blue and red cats and dogs all over them, her graying hair pulled back in a low pony tail. She doesn't even look up as she scribbles some notes onto a clipboard.

We hang up our jackets on a hook near the door and I roll up my sleeves as I walk past the glass windows that allow visitors to view the cat enclosures. Two adorable calico kittens paw at the window, and I pause to put my hand up against their paws. They'll be adopted. The kittens always are.

Nick holds open the swinging door and I follow him into the kennel areas. The dogs start barking again and it rings in my ears as we pass each of the kennels.

It's always sad to know that the dogs I see today will be gone by the time I return next week. Adopted or put down, whichever is their fate. I stopped asking what happened to them after the first two weeks. All that matters is that we're giving them a nice spa treatment to better their chances of finding homes.

The last door on the left leads into a big wash room with two low sinks. I take a deep breath and swing open the door, the steamy warmth greeting me. We each grab an apron, and I end up with the one with goofy poodles all over it. I slip it over my head, pulling my hair out of the way, then turn around. Nick's fingers graze the bare skin above the waistband of my jeans as he ties the strings in a bow. I blink. It's nothing out of the ordinary, so why am I so aware of it?

"Come on, I think I saw a big drooling mastiff out there with your name on it," I say. Nick gives me a little shove on the shoulder, and I grin and bump my hip into his.

We end up with the mastiff and a mangy looking labradoodle, which has matted, tangled fir. Nick easily lifts the labradoodle into the sink and ties her leash onto a cleat, and then we stare at the gigantic mastiff. Its head reaches my hip.

"Uh, I call the front end." I maneuver around to the front, but one look at the long strings of drool changes my mind. "On second thought…"

I look up at Nick and we both burst out laughing. "It looks like it swallowed a whole bowl of spaghetti and the noodles are still hanging out," I say.

"I can probably get him."

Nick loops his arms around the body of the dog and grunts as he picks it up; the mastiff must weigh at least a hundred and twenty pounds. The dog flails around a little as Nick dumps it into the big washbasin. I step forward to cinch its leash down just as it shakes it head again, big jowls flapping around. A chunk of saliva dislodges and lands on the chest of my apron. I blink. Ugh, this is disgusting.

Nick grabs a towel and reaches over to wipe it off, but just as the towel touches my chest, he freezes and a blush spreads across his cheeks. "Uh, here," he says, thrusting it at me.

I blink, brushing past him as I go to my sink and wet the labradoodle down with the hose, staring at the wall instead of Nick. "How'd you do on your senior project?"

Silence greets me. He must have nodded or shrugged or something. I twist around and look back at him.

"Aced it."

Yes, of course. "Nice. I got a B-, because I dropped my cards halfway through and mixed them up and jumped around in the speech."

"That sucks."

I glance back at him. His back is to me as he leans over the basin, vigorously scrubbing the mastiff. Apron strings are tied loosely around his waist, and as he leans further over, his T-shirt stretches over the muscles in his back. Nick's not the same scrawny guy I befriended so many years ago. Maybe he's still on the awkward side—the

43

total opposite of that casual confidence in Carter—but he's filled out, so he's not so gangly any more.

Not that I could ever find the courage to tell him that.

A small stereo mounted under one of the supply cabinets streams out a quiet hum of classic rock. I turn back to the labradoodle and reach for the bottle of soap, squirting a long line of the pinky goop down the dog's back. Just as I cap the shampoo, setting it on the ledge beside the basin, warm water blasts me on the back of the neck. I twist around, put my hands up to shield myself, but it makes it worse. The water hits my hand and ricochets upward, getting me on the face.

"Argh!" I storm toward him and Nick steps back, but the wall is behind him. He uses the nozzle as a deterrent, a heavy stream aimed right at my chest, but I yank the nozzle out of his hands and stand inches from him, the hose pointed right at his face.

"Give me one reason I shouldn't nail you with this," I say, one side of my mouth turned up in a smug smile.

"Uh, because we're best friends?"

"Try harder," I say, inching the nozzle closer.

"Because there's no honor in a close-range assassination?"

I just grin wider and pull the trigger. Water splays everywhere as he grabs the nozzle and my wrists and wrestles the hose from my hands. We twist around and soon I'm pinned against the wall, the hose between us. Nick steps closer, leans in, a wicked smile on his face.

"Let's try this again," he says.

I cringe and close my eyes, waiting for the cold shock of the water, but it doesn't come.

Instead, it's the soft warmth of Nick's lips on mine. The air leaves my lungs all at once, the world tilting.

This can't be real.

My chest burns, but I keep my eyes closed as I hear the hose clatter to the floor, feel Nick's hands on my face, pulling me closer.

When he retreats I take in a ragged breath of air, but I leave my eyes closed.

I just kissed Nick.

Nick just kissed *me*.

I shut my eyes tighter, afraid when I open them that I'll be in my bed at home, that this was all in my imagination.

I hear the water spray again, and I blink my eyes open. Nick has his back to me and is at his washbasin again. I stand there until he looks back at me, meets my eyes for a long, lingering moment filled with such intensity it's hard not to look away. I feel like he's *reading* me.

"What was that?"

He blushes and looks back at the washbasin. He's not getting off that easy. I walk up beside him and put a hand on the nozzle so he has to stop perpetually rinsing the dog. "Nick?"

He meets my eyes, shrugging as a shy smile pulls at his lips. "Sorry. I just... wanted to know."

"Know what?"

"If kissing you would be as good as I thought it would be."

The air leaves my lungs. "And?"

His smile grows, his blue eyes turning warm as he stares down at me from his towering six-foot-three height. "It was."

I blink. I want to ask him a thousand things but I can't articulate any of them. Nick kissed me. *Nick*.

He turns back to the washbasin. "I lied to you. I didn't sleep with Reyna. We broke up for good a month ago."

"Why?"

He squeezes the nozzle again for a minute. "Because she didn't like how much I talked about you."

"Oh."

I'm not entirely sure I heard him correctly over my thundering heart. This is the sort of conversation I've heard inside my head. About 9,532 times.

He stares at the dog for a long moment before looking at me again, those deep blue eyes sincere. He's not screwing with me. "I won't kiss you again if you don't want me to."

I furrow my brows. "I don't—" I gulp. I want him to kiss me. I want him to want to kiss me. I want this to be something, so desperately that it hurts.

"Okay," he says, nodding.

"That wasn't the whole sentence," I say.

He twists around and rests his hip against the washbasin, staring me dead in the eye and waiting.

"I mean, I don't want you to … *not* kiss me."

Jeez, I'm screwing this up.

"Kiss me again," I say.

"What?"

"Kiss me again." I wring my hands together. I don't have to ask a third time. Nick takes my face in his hands and pulls me closer, his eyes open this time, boring into mine. He stops just a fraction of an inch from my lips, tantalizingly close, and the moment stretches on for what seems like eternity, sparks jumping between us.

But he doesn't kiss me. He just stays like that, our lips a breath apart, but so far away.

And then I throw my arms around his shoulders and yank him against me, closing my eyes as I kiss him.

As his tongue grazes my lower lip, I feel weak. I tighten my arms around his shoulders to keep my knees from buckling.

He's right. It's just as good as I thought it would be.

Four

When we turn the corner, I see that Dad's home. His dark blue Dodge Charger, complete with blue-and-red lights and *POLICE* paint job, is parked in our drive.

There are only two cops in all of Mossyrock. My dad, and a thirty-seven-year-old guy named Russ. That's it. The whole police force. My dad has worked for the department since he was twenty-four, which gives him seniority and the practically automatic title of Police Chief.

He grew up in this town. At one time, he wanted out. He wanted to see the world, be somebody outside of this stupid place that seems to trap people. So he joined the army and did a couple of tours, and eventually found himself in sunny San Diego.

And that's where he met my mom, Julianna. She was pretty, all long blond hair and tanned skin. Not that I remember, but I've seen the pictures.

They fell in love, and, from what little I can gather, Dad thought it would be happily ever after. Dad got transferred to Europe, and they got married so she could go with him.

But a year later she was over it. Over him. They broke up and she went back home.

And then she found out she was pregnant with me. About the same time, Dad's contract with the army was up and Mossyrock was hiring a cop. He convinced her this small town was the best place to raise a kid. Dad bought a little house, and the two of them settled in his old hometown, but it was never enough for my mom. She hung around for a while, had a baby, got restless, and left him again. Except this time, she left me too.

It's been the two of us ever since. Dad kept the house, kept the job, and kept me, and nothing has changed in seventeen years. And if I don't go away for college, nothing will change in the next seventeen either.

Nick pulls his Mustang into the driveway of his house, switches it off, and we fall silent. Silence is normally comfortable with us, but I'm not sure either of us know how to act right now. "See you tomorrow?" he asks.

I twist away from staring at the window and meet his eyes. "Yeah. Sounds good."

He smiles, and before I can take a breath, he leans over, brushes his lips against mine, and then sits back and unbuckles his seat belt. "Cool. See you then."

I nod and unclick my seat belt, my heart in my throat. Three. Three kisses in one day.

I have to force my limbs to move so that I can get out of his car. "Uh, later," I say, starting to walk away.

"Sam?"

I twist around.

"You forgot your purse."

"Oh. Uh, right." I feel my cheeks flush with heat as I lean down and grab my purse from the floorboards. I wave goodbye, striding across the lawn as I hear Nick's front door click shut.

"Dad, I'm home," I call out, once inside. I hang my purse up on the hook by the door and put my shoes into the basket. *A place for everything and everything in its place.*

"In here," he calls back.

I make my way to the kitchen, my socks silent on the hardwood floors, and find my dad at a stool reading the newspaper, an iced tea sweating on a coaster beside him.

"Having a good day?" he asks, not looking up from the paper.

"Uh-huh. You?" I walk to the fridge and pull out a Diet Coke, cracking the top as I walk to the cupboard and grab a bag of chips. I set the coke down and pop a Dorito in my mouth.

"That stuff's not healthy," he says, finally looking up at me. As if iced tea is any better.

"Then why do you buy it?"

He seems to barely suppress the urge to roll his eyes. "I picked up the catalog from CCC today."

The chips suddenly taste like chalk. "But I told you I don't want to go to Centralia Community College."

"It's a perfectly reasonable choice. If you don't register soon, the good classes will be filled."

"But you know I got into UW ..." *And I already picked my classes*, I mentally add.

"And you can go in a year or two, when your core classes are done and you have the maturity it takes to go to school in a big city."

"Seattle isn't that big, Dad. Mossyrock is just—"

"End of discussion." He closes his newspaper and stands. "Keep arguing and you're grounded."

I can only stare as he saunters down the hall. Then I toss the whole bag of chips into the garbage.

Five

At seven forty on a normal Monday morning, I'm sluggish. But today, as I walk past the junior high building, heading for the high school front doors, I feel strangely bouncy.

Nick kissed me yesterday. *I* kissed *him*. What was that? Will it happen again? That second kiss, when he came so tantalizingly close but made me close the gap, was the sexiest thing I could have imagined. He wanted *me* to make the choice.

A thousand thoughts rolled through my head all night long, keeping me up so late I should feel tired and dragging, but I can't help the adrenaline that flows through me as I bounce through the doors.

When I'm only a few steps into the bustling halls of MHS, something shifts. The back of my neck prickles. I grip my can of Diet Coke harder, walk a little slower, and try to look around without bobbing my head left and right. My Mary Janes seem ridiculously loud in the carpeted hall.

The energy I had moments before turns to sludge in my veins. It's like those movies where everyone is talking in hushed whispers, and then someone walks into the room and everything goes silent.

I am that someone. Groups of students huddle around their lockers, some using the doors to obscure their lips as they lean in, whispering, their eyes never leaving my face. My cheeks burn as I hustle past them, feeling the warmth of a thousand sets of eyes. The hall suddenly seems longer than ever, my locker impossibly far away.

I get this weird feeling, like everyone knows about Nick and me and thinks it's just as newsworthy as I do, but I dismiss it. Half this school thinks Nick and I have been a couple for the last two years, no matter what we say to dispel the rumor. No one would care if we got together. No one would *stare*.

I keep walking, staring straight ahead, acting as if I don't notice the way everyone seems to swivel toward me as I pass. But the further I walk, the more hushed the hall becomes, like a veil of silence is falling over everyone all at once. There's a group of seniors leaning back against the big windows that line the walls, and they all pause and watch me as I pass. I suddenly wonder if I covered my bruise well enough. It's got a bluish look to it now, and it was harder to hide. Do I look like I fell down and my face broke my fall?

But then something else—something worse—occurs to me.

Carter told.

Carter told everyone that I threw myself at him, and they all had a good laugh at my expense.

I hope he didn't include the two-bagger part.

I dig into my purse, grab my sunglasses, and shove them on, even though it's a little too dark in here to wear them. I bought them at a street fair almost a year ago and they're vying for least-fashionable thing I own, which is a pretty big feat considering the clothes in my closet.

But it makes it easier to pretend I don't see the way time slows down, don't see the way every set of eyes in the room swivels in my direction, only to dart away in the worst possible way, as if afraid to be caught looking at me.

The sudden attention is unnerving. I'm hyper-aware of every joint and muscle in my body, and suddenly it's like I have to tell my feet to move properly.

Why did I have to go to that stupid party? Why did I have to go into Carter's room? Nick knew it was a bad idea. Tried to talk me out of it. I should have listened. But it must be a light day for gossip if people thinking Carter's rejection of me is *this* big of a deal. I wonder if he embellished the insults, made them especially comical.

I navigate the wide, crowded halls and get to my ugly, gray-painted locker. My hand is shaking so badly I can barely unlock it. It takes me three tries. Three torturous tries. All I want to do is flee to first period, where no one will be because it doesn't start for another ten minutes.

I manage to open the door and grab my English and math books, the only ones I'll need before first break.

When I slam the door shut, I nearly jump out of my skin.

Veronica Michaels is standing in front of me, barely ten inches away. We used to be friends, back in freshman year, but she's managed to climb the social ladder while I'm still down here with the little people. In class, we have this unspoken agreement not to partner up on anything, not to sit too near each other.

Which is practically impossible in a school this small. Every year, we have at least two out of seven classes together.

"Are you okay?" she asks.

I scrunch my eyebrows. "Um … yes?"

Why is she talking to me? Is she relishing my fall from grace? Is Carter laughing at me really that big of a deal? Is it the two-bagger part everyone finds so amusing? Or is it just because people think a loser like me actually tried to hook up with him?

She gets this little frowny face that reminds me of the expression you'd give someone if you found out their puppy died. Lips turned down, eyebrows furrowed, eyes all crinkled-up. "You swear?"

"Uhh . . . yeah."

She gets this really weird, intense look on her face. Considering she's got massive glittery eye shadow, it looks a little funny. It's weird to think I was friends with her once, because this girl? I barely recognize her.

She leans in, so close I think I can smell the strawberry Pop-Tart she had for breakfast. "Is it true?"

"Is what true?" My heart climbs further into my throat. This *is* about the party . . . isn't it? My eyes dart around, like somehow I'll *see* what the hell it is everyone's talking about. Like there'll be this big sign that says, "Yo, Student Body! Samantha Marshall is a virgin!"

Oh God. What if he told everyone I'm not? What if he said we slept together or that I was *willing* to sleep with him? It wasn't like that at all. I was just using him to get Nick.

I glance around again, quickly confirm that I'm still the focus of half the people in this hallway. I try to figure out what kind of a rumor Carter might have started that could be this newsworthy. But I'm not sure I really want to know.

It's easier to look at Veronica, because now I'm sure I'm right. People really are staring at me. People who didn't glance my way last week.

Veronica takes this low, deep breath and leans in even closer. Now I swear I can smell the *sprinkles* on the Pop-Tart. "About Carter Wellesley . . . in his bedroom . . . last Friday?"

The air whooshes out of my lungs until I'm pretty sure they've collapsed in on themselves. I can't get any oxygen anymore because the edges of my vision are a little fuzzy and dark.

He totally did tell everyone I went after him, and I bet he exaggerated.

Is that why this is such a big deal? Because no one sees me as that kind of girl, and they're all shocked, thinking I'd go that far?

Veronica is still staring at me. All I can smell is artificial strawberry.

"Oh, um…" I run my hands through my hair. I look away from her, and all I see are a hundred sets of eyes still burning into me. Then I nod. "Uh, kinda. Just, please… don't tell anyone, okay?"

It's stupid, because obviously he's already bragged to half the freaking school. How could he do that? Are they all amazed that mousy little Samantha Marshall was willing to put out? Was drinking?

I wish I could rewind, undo everything I did, especially since I never had to go for Carter at all. Nick broke up with Reyna a month ago. He was thinking about what it was like to kiss *me*.

The whole thing with Carter was a mistake.

What if Nick hears the rumor that I slept with Carter and no longer wants me? I feel sick. What if the very thing I tried to do to get Nick is the thing that makes me lose him?

Veronica wraps her arms around me so abruptly I don't have time to react. Just a quick hug, and then she steps back. The perkiness created by her extreme makeup completely disappears when I see the soft, caring look in her eyes.

Confusion twists through me. She feels sorry for me? Maybe she feels bad that everyone thinks I gave up the V-card to Carter at a party. Everyone says she's a man-hater, so I guess that makes sense.

"I'm here if you need anything, okay? I mean, I know that sounds stupid or something since we haven't talked much the last few years, but you don't deserve … that."

I nod, but I don't know what to say to her. Instead, I just turn away, look at the faces staring back at me.

And then I blink; it's Nick walking toward me, an adorable half-smile on his face, and everyone else vanishes.

"I'll catch up with you later," I say, walking away from her.

"Hey," Nick says, leaning in to give me a hug. His scent washes over me, something fresh, like Ivory Soap.

"Hi."

"How's your morning going?" he asks as we turn toward our joint English class.

"Oh, you know, the usual." I make a vague sweeping motion with my hand. What if Nick wants to know why everyone is staring? What if he hears the rumors? It could ruin everything.

"I didn't sleep well at all last night," Nick says, reaching out for my hand. I let him interweave our fingers as a warmth floods my insides. I want to stare at our hands, but instead it's everything I can do to just walk normally, keep from looking robotic and unnatural as my best friend holds my hand.

"Why not?"

He catches my eye and grins. "You."

"Oh," I say, flushing.

"We should go out this week. Do something…
different."

"Dinner?"

He shrugs. "Maybe. Or a movie."

I try to keep breathing. There's no movie theater in
Mossyrock. There's no bowling alley, or miniature golf, or
anything. We'll have to go to Morton or Chehalis or something. "Like a date?"

"Yeah," he says, squeezing my hand. This all feels surreal, like I'm watching it play out in my head while lying
in bed late at night, dreaming it all up.

"Sounds good."

We're at the door to our English class and drop hands
as we enter. Which is probably good, because if it had lasted
much longer, I'm sure my palm would sweat profusely.

I plunk down in my chair beside Nick and wonder
how I can handle sitting so close to him, when everything
is changing and all I want to do is be alone with him.

———

Nick and I share the first two classes of the day—English
first, and then math right across the hall—but after that,
we go separate ways. Once we're apart, I can't stop noticing
the stares during class, the whispers in the halls—or worse,
the weird silence. Panic creeps in, because I still haven't figured out exactly what everyone is talking about … and I'm

worried that in the last few hours, Nick *has* figured it out, and it could be bad. Really bad.

I round the corner and jerk to a stop, seeing Carter up ahead with two of his friends. His buddies are leaning back against the lockers, and Carter is standing with his back to the students streaming past him.

I take a backward step, then another, unable to take my eyes off of him. Part of me wants to march up and ask him what he told everyone, but I know I don't have the guts to. If bravery was my strong suit, I wouldn't be in this position to begin with.

Someone in a ball cap rams into Carter, nearly knocking him off his feet. Carter regains his balance and whirls around. "What the hell is your problem, man?"

The guy flips him off over his shoulder and just keeps walking. That's weird. I thought everyone liked Carter.

Carter turns back to his friends and I spin around, hoping he didn't catch a glimpse of me, and scurry off in the other direction. I'll take the roundabout way to the cafeteria. I'll grab something to eat and bail, go eat on the front lawn or something.

Mossyrock only has two lunch periods: one for the junior high, one for the high school. The two schools share faculty, the office, the cafeteria. It's a joint campus, basically.

Which means Carter has this lunch break too, and so does Nick.

People part as I pass by, and by the time I make it to the lunchroom, I'm almost running. I beat the majority of the crowd and snag a spot in line behind a half-dozen other students.

Why did I have to drink so much? Why, why, *why*? Sometimes Dad's rules are stupid, but it's true that nothing like this has ever happened to me when I followed them.

I just want to go home, but I have a Spanish test. It's stupid, too. About traveling—airplanes and luggage. Like I'm heading off to Spain any time soon. Please. Dad would never, in a million years, let me go abroad. I could win an all-expenses-paid trip and he'd still forbid it.

No, I'll be spending the summer right here in Mossy-rock, waiting for August to arrive so I can run off to UW and finally escape my dad's hawk eyes.

I'm fidgeting, tapping my feet on the floor as the line creeps forward, when Tracey walks up to me, all golden-blond perfection.

Tracey, ex-girlfriend of one Carter Wellesley.

Shit. She must have heard about … whatever people think happened. If everyone thinks I slept with him and they only broke up two weeks ago, she's gotta be ticked. She's probably going to deck me. Tear me from limb to limb. She's on the volleyball team and tough as hell, despite being the perfect girly sort of girl.

She ignores everyone around us and leans in close. "Did he really do that?"

Did he do *what*? Laugh at me? Sleep with me and brag about it?

Her perfect, almond-colored eyes are narrowed, but they look more concerned than angry. I don't get it.

I swallow, pretend she must be talking to someone else, and just keep staring at the back of the head of the person in front of me in line.

She lowers her voice. "I mean, he was always kind of an asshole ..."

Wait, what?

So he must have walked out of his room and, like, told everyone at the party I threw myself at him or something. But wouldn't Nick have heard that? I pick up lunch tray from the stack and then stare down at the stainless steel counter as I slide my ugly, plastic green tray along. *Please, just leave me alone.*

"Sam."

I jerk my head up.

"Is it true?"

What do I do now? Tell her I don't know the answer because I don't even understand the question? She needs to go away. All of this just needs to go away

I don't look at her as I nod my head slowly, happy that at least there's not a lump in my throat right now. I don't even know why she's talking to me. They broke up.

She lets out a string of curses I hadn't even thought she was capable of. "Damn it! He is such an asshole!"

People are staring again. God, I hope Carter doesn't walk in right now. I glance around, surveying the growing crowd for his letterman jacket or for Nick's head of dark wavy hair, the trapped feeling intensifying in my stomach.

"Come here," she says, yanking me by the elbow out

of line. My plastic tray, completely devoid of food, is left behind on the counter. I guess this day really can get worse.

She pulls me into the corner. I see her nod at someone else, and before I know it, Macy, her petite, dark-haired best friend, is joining us. Can't they see I don't want any of this?

They edge closer, like they're about to share their secret handshake for being popular. But they don't. Instead, Tracey says, "He dumped me because I slept with him."

Her revelation is so unexpected that I jerk back, nearly smacking my head on the puke-green cinderblock behind me. *Huh?* Why is she telling me this? This is like, top-secret A-lister stuff, not things she should tell the peons like me.

Macy's eyes widen but it's like she's trying to look sympathetic, not surprised. "And he dumped me because I *wouldn't.* Total dickhead, completely pushy. Had to shove him off me before he got the point, and then he called me frigid."

What? I can't fathom why these girls are talking to me, let alone sharing this information. Are we supposed to be bonding over our mutual hatred of Carter? Join some I-Hate-Carter club?

"I know this is weird," Tracey says. *You think?* "But we just wanted you to know we're here for you, okay? Anything you need."

Macy nods. "Totally. You are *so brave* for coming to school today."

"*So brave,*" Tracey adds.

How come all I can think is, *huh?* I just nod and shrug and do whatever noncommittal thing I can.

Tracey and Macy, which rhymes, now that I think about it, saunter off and leave me alone to the wolves, who stare and drool, salivating over whatever gossip they can discern.

I can't take this anymore. I don't want to explain this to Nick, I don't want to see Carter, and I don't want to feel like a spectacle any longer. I don't even understand what is happening, let alone what I should do about it.

I rush off to the bathroom, shoving my way through a crowd of people who can't stop staring.

Six

I've been sitting in the handicapped stall of the bathroom for at least an hour. My legs are tingly and numb, but I can't seem to care enough to move. I assume that my fourth-period class has continued on without me.

It won't matter, though. I'm never absent, and it's History, my second-best class of the day after English. Mr. Hawk won't mark me absent even if I'm not there. He'll convince himself I'm in the library working on an extra-credit piece I don't need.

Besides, Carter's in that class. I need to know what he's been telling everyone before I can figure out what I want to say to him.

Study hall is starting soon, and I really should leave this bathroom, yet I can't get myself to move. I keep picturing myself pushing the bathroom door open and seeing an entire cafeteria full of classmates sitting there, staring right at the door, waiting for me to emerge. Then they all stand up and start shouting things at me all at once, like some kind of press conference that features only questions I can't answer.

I should just go find Veronica. Tell her I don't know what everyone is talking about, why they are all so interested in me when all that really happened was Carter laughing at me. She can fill in the details, tell me what the rumors are. But I'm afraid to walk out because I don't want to be in the halls by myself. I don't even know where she is right now.

So I just keep sitting on the toilet, pants up and fully buttoned, my temple resting on the divider wall. It's probably crawling with germs, but I don't care.

The bathroom door swings open and footsteps shuffle in, echoing in that way only bathrooms do. I close my eyes and take in a long, quiet breath. I wish they hadn't disturbed my sanctuary.

"I don't know, I wasn't there. That's just what I heard," a girl's voice says. She sounds really young. Fourteen or so. And she has a hint of a lisp. "He only invites upperclassmen to his parties," she adds. She sounds envious. Like she spends all of her time dreaming of said parties.

"That's so crazy, though," a higher-pitched voice responds. "Carter Wellesley? Are you sure?"

My mouth goes dry. Can I not get some peace? Even the *freshmen* know about me? For a second I want to bolt. Storm out in a huff. But then I realize … maybe I can figure out what everyone *thinks* happened. Every part of me freezes and my breathing turns shallow. They can't know I'm here.

It's silent for a second as they stop in front of the mirror. I'm surprised they haven't figured out someone is in here, because the stall door is shut. My heart beats so hard I imagine it tick-tocks like the telltale heart.

I can just see their feet and the frayed cuffs of their jeans. One of them is wearing black Converse with white stars, and the other has on brown leather ballet flats.

I imagine Converse girl nodding, eyes wide, enjoying the juicy gossip.

"Who was the victim?" asks ballet flats girl.

Victim? Why would they call me that? My mind flies to the pink mark on my cheek, which I spent ten minutes covering. But what if I didn't do a good job?

Oh God. What if everyone thinks Carter *hit me*? Is that what this is about?

"Some girl named Samantha," I hear the first girl say. "I looked her up in the yearbook. Total geek, chess club or something. She even has glasses."

Had glasses. I got contacts over the summer. And I'm not a geek. I'm not in the chess club, either. I'm not in *any* club. All I really like to do is write, and no one even knows I do that.

One of them flips the water on for a second and then

switches it off again. I hear the sounds of a compact opening and closing. Are they actually powdering their noses? Who does that?

"Still," ballet flats girl argues, "Carter is so freakin' hot, he could sleep with anyone he wants. If he wanted to sleep with someone like her, she'd fall at his feet. There's no way he'd have to rape her."

Rape me?

The nausea that has been rising all day chokes me all at once. I concentrate on breathing through my nose, my fingernails digging into my jeans, as the whole bathroom spins and tilts on its side. Every moment of the morning rushes in front of me, like an entire movie played on fast-forward . . .

The stares. The questions. The "Is it true?" The things Tracey and Macy told me. "He got really pushy with me," she'd said, giving me a sympathetic pat. Like I was supposed to get it or something. Someone egged Carter's car yesterday. Someone else shoulder-checked him this morning in the hall. Was it because of this?

No. *No.* They can't think that. They just can't. It's not what happened. Carter rejected me. Laughed at me. He didn't do *that.*

The two girls' conversation dies out as the door swings shut behind them, and then I'm kneeling, retching up nothingness since my stomach is already empty.

The entire school thinks I was raped.

By Carter.

I grip the edges of the hard plastic toilet seat, resting

my forehead on my knees as I continue to squat like that in the dingy bathroom stall.

How can I go back out there? They think Carter raped me—Carter Wellesley, the guy they all love, all flirt with, all admire. The guy they want to either be or be with.

There's just no way they'd believe it.

My face flames hotter. I don't want to talk to anyone right now, I want to burrow into a giant hole and never come out.

Oh God, and Carter … if it's this bad for me, what is everyone saying to him? What kind of looks are they giving him? He's the god of the senior class. Everyone worships the ground he walks on. And he didn't do it. But everyone thinks he did, and I unknowingly went along with it, and it's all a lie. People must be looking at him. Questioning him … judging him for something he never did.

I stand up so fast everything spins again and I have to put a hand up against the stall.

I have to get out of here. I can't handle seeing him right now, him thinking I made this up and am spreading the lie myself, like I'm spiteful or something about his rejection. I want to punch him in the nose, not accuse him of rape.

I slam my way out of the stall, the door bouncing so hard it ricochets twice, and I bound right out the bathroom door, scurrying down the halls with my heart in my throat, praying no one sees me. I don't know what happens if you skip school, but I don't want to find out either.

I glance over as I pass my locker, and then trip on my own feet.

Whore.

It's etched in angry, jagged writing, a stark black against the gray paint. I stumble over to it, try to rub it off with my fingers, but it's permanent marker. My chest tightens as I turn away, desperate to leave this place, leave the imprint of that word behind.

If they think he raped me, why would they write that? *Who* would write that?

I keep my head down, hoping no one stops me along the way. I make it out to the parking lot. Thirty feet to freedom. Thirty feet to the sanctuary of my seven-year-old, lemon-yellow Ford Focus.

And then a girl's face looms into my vision and I stumble back. Wavy red hair. Bright green eyes framed by eggshell glasses. Freckled skin.

Gina Berkeley, a girl in my Spanish and math classes. I jerk away.

Her eyes widen but neither of us speak. At least, not for a long, stifling moment. And then she says, "I'm not surprised."

Her voice is flat, unemotional. It doesn't fit the girl who was always so bubbly as she conjugated verbs.

"By?"

"Carter."

A lump grows in my throat. I don't want to talk about this, I just want out.

"He's a horrible human being. Did you know I asked

him out once?" Those beautiful green eyes start to glitter. "He just seemed ... down to earth, you know? Such a gorgeous, perfect exterior, and yet he somehow seemed approachable. Like I wasn't completely mental to think I had a chance."

I nod. Because there's nothing else to do.

"He was with two friends when I walked up to him. It wasn't like I threw myself at his feet or something. I just asked if he wanted to get together to study for the big trig final. I mean God, I had three years of math with him. All the way back to junior high. We weren't strangers." She tightens her lips and looks up at the clouds for a moment before looking back at me. "And you want to know what he said?"

No. No, I don't want to know what he said. Because I know what he said. I can see where she's coming from a mile away. And it's not some kind of easy landing. It's a complete crash and burn. An explosion of flames so consuming it's still burning her, a year later.

"He got really serious. Leaned in and motioned me closer. And then told me he had a vision problem."

I furrow my brow, confused, as she gets a faraway look in her eyes. Carter doesn't wear glasses.

"Because he couldn't *see* spending more than four seconds in my presence, because I was about as pleasant to look at as a donkey's ass."

I choke, then. The lump in my throat thickens into a boulder. Her eyes get a glimmery, jewel-like look to them as she blinks rapidly. "His friends laughed so hard they could barely breathe. One of them bent over and started slapping the wall, and they just kept laughing, and laughing, and laughing. I was so mortified I couldn't seem to move. I just stood there while they laughed at me."

Her lips tremble, and she swallows. But like me, it's not enough to clear the pain away. "When I heard what he did to you…"

I part my lips but can't speak. Because he *didn't* do what she thinks he did. What everyone thinks he did. The giant boulder—no, mountain—in my throat seems to block all ability to speak.

"I wasn't surprised. He's the most self-centered, ego-driven, jerk of a guy I've ever met. I'm just sorry you had to go through—"

"I don't really want to talk about it," I say. "I'm sorry for … for what he did to you."

I don't give her a chance to respond, I just flee.

Seven

I make it home before one fifteen, and then I land some-where underneath the heavy comforter in my bedroom, and all I can seem to do is burrow in. Deeper and deeper I go, but it's not enough to escape reality. I want a hole to open up and yank me in. A caved-in mining shaft, where no one will ever try to rescue me.

I close my eyes and try to go back to Friday night. It's all fuzzy, like I'm viewing it through a pair of out-of-focus binoculars. I remember sitting there in those pinching high heels, sipping nonstop on the beer just to give myself something to do. I kept glancing around, wondering if my plan could really work. Wondering where Nick went off to. Wondering why I always had to be the outsider while everyone surrounding me was having such a great time.

How am I going to walk into school tomorrow morning and tell everyone he didn't do it? I have to. I know that. Carter might not be the perfect guy I thought he was—in fact, turns out he might just be the biggest asshole I've ever met—but I can't wreck his life with one obliterating lie.

It's not like *I* lied. Not exactly. Michelle, at the party, obviously jumped to her own conclusions. I nodded, I remember that, when she was talking. I didn't know what she said, but I nodded.

And … now? Everyone thinks *I said* he did it. And somehow, maybe I did, when I agreed with Veronica, let her hug me. When I stood with Macy and Tracey and accepted their condolences.

All day long, I confirmed everything they said.

Everyone thinks he really did it. That he … socked me in the face? Ripped my clothes? Forced himself on me? Do they all really believe Carter is capable of that?

And that's when I remember the egg yolk dripping down his car. Remember Michelle's text on Saturday. They *do* believe it. The rumor had all weekend to rage unchecked. All weekend to make the rounds. How did Nick dodge it? Why did no one tell him. … or me?

I sink deeper into my soft feather pillow and let out a soul-ravaging sigh. I really screwed this up. The drapes in my room are pulled shut so tight all I can see are shadows on the popcorn ceiling. I close my eyes and pray for it all to disappear.

I don't think I fall asleep. In fact, I'm certain I've spent no more than two minutes with my eyes shut when I'm jarred upright by the doorbell. I gulp hard, and then my hands yank back the blanket. Fully dressed. Of course I'm dressed, I never got *undressed.* I glance at the clock: 1:33 p.m.

The doorbell chimes, over and over and over again, obnoxious. I don't want to get out of bed, but the chiming is incessant, nonstop.

I creep down the hall, the glossy hardwoods creaking under my feet. The chiming continues. *Bing Bing Bing Bing.*

What if it's Carter? What is he's out there fuming, wanting revenge? He must be furious right now. I creep up to the door, the cold of the hardwoods leaching into my socks. Then I lean in, slowly, to peek through the peephole.

Nick. Relief whooshes through me, but it doesn't last more than a moment. He's standing there, agitated, his arms crossing and uncrossing as he punches the doorbell. His Mustang is parked crookedly and carelessly at the curb.

I step back, not sure if I want to open the door. Figuratively and literally.

I need him. He's the only person in the world I trust, and the only one who can make my head stop spinning. I need him to understand how I never meant for any of this to happen.

I need him to fix it.

I glance back through the peephole. He's pacing now. Every time he passes the door, he reaches out, punches the doorbell, and then spins around, stalks in the opposite direction, and repeats the process. Stalk, *bing*, spin, stalk, *bing*, spin, stalk, *bing*…

He knows I'm here because my car is parked at the curb, in front of his, a light sheen of raindrops gracing the surface.

There's no getting out of this. I take in a long, deep breath, and then swing the door open.

Nick bursts into the foyer and reels around on me. "I've tried to call you at least twenty times in the last half hour," he says, his voice razor-thin. "Brian Merrimont asked me how you were doing at lunch, looking all concerned. I had no idea what he was talking about." His words are coming out so fast it's hard to discern what he's saying. "And then he tells me what he heard on Saturday, after the party, about how you—" He chokes on his words and spins on me. "It's not true. Tell me it's not true."

My lips part but I'm so shocked by his outburst—by calm, cool, diplomatic Nick—that I end up just staring at him.

"It has to be a lie. You would have said something to me over the weekend if he did that. Plus, I played pool with Carter until two in the morning and he was acting totally normal." He's … frantic. Crazed. "You're my best friend. I would know if it were true, so it can't be."

"What?"

Nick hasn't stopped his pacing, even though he's inside now. "How could he have done that to you? How could it have happened and you didn't even tell me?"

He's not even looking at me, just pacing, and I have the strangest feeling that I could retreat down the hall and he'd still keep talking, because it's like he's talking to himself.

But then he turns to me. "Why are you lying?" His voice goes an octave higher than I ever thought it could.

He's totally melting down. Pain twists inside me, mingles with confusion. How can he do this? I need him to be the rock he always is. I need him to swoop in just like always and fix things. When my dad makes me cry, Nick's the one who makes it disappear. When my car got a flat, Nick was the one to change it so I wouldn't have to tell Dad his stupid flat-tire lesson didn't sink in. When I nearly flunked math, Nick was the one who tutored me.

And maybe it is a lie, but *I* never lied. I chew on the inside of my cheek and try to keep from falling apart just like him. "I didn't lie," I say, with difficulty. I didn't. *I didn't lie.*

He throws up his hands. "I don't think Carter would do that!"

And then I explode right back, my hands fisted up so that I won't rip out my own hair. "Do you even know who Carter is?" If he did, he never would have let me walk into his house. He would have known what could happen and he would have protected me from the humiliation.

"I've had classes with him for twelve years, the same as you! Of course I know him!"

"Just because you sit next to him in Chemistry doesn't mean you know him!" I scream, surprising even myself.

How did it come to this? Yesterday he kissed me, this

morning we held hands, and now he's screaming at me. I think I have whiplash.

"It can't be true! It can't be!"

I'm ashamed and angry and disappointed and embarrassed all at once. Nick knows it's not true. Does he think I'm lying, that I went out and told people Carter did that? I want to burst into tears and scream out loud. Why can't he just stop yelling? Why does he have to turn on me just like everyone else?

Why doesn't *anyone* ever just be reliable and be there for me?

I don't even notice the tears at first until they're shimmering so hard I can't see and suddenly it's hard to breath and I barely make it to the carpeted stairs in time to collapse.

I just want one person. *One* person to be there consistently.

This is the worst day of my life. Here he is, demanding I tell the truth, but he hasn't asked me what the truth is. If he'd just asked me, I would have told him what happened. Would have begged him to understand how it all spiraled out of control before I even knew what was going on.

I pull my legs up underneath me and buckle over, curling into myself and crying so hard my shoulders wrack. Carter thinks I'm so ugly he'd need two bags ... the guys on his team think I'm a slut ... and the rest of the school thinks I'm a charity case. And if anyone hadn't heard the rumor yet, the word *whore* emblazoned on my locker ensures they know about it now.

And now, after the first kiss to ever make me feel something, Nick is going to hate me.

My nose drips with snot as the tears turn my jeans wet. I'm shaking so hard it rattles my lungs.

And then there's Nick, his arms wrapping around my shoulders. He pulls me into him, rubs his hand soothingly on the back of my neck, as if smoothing my long blond hair free of knots. The sobs don't lessen at first, but soon I hear him whispering and have to force my cries to quiet so I can hear his words.

"I'm sorry. I shouldn't have yelled at you like that."

His hand rubs so softly up and down my back I can hardly feel it. "I know you're right. I don't really know him. I've heard things about him in the locker rooms, but I just didn't want to think he'd go this far. Oh God, I'm so sorry I wasn't there. Are you okay?"

Somehow his arms around me are enough to bring the world back under control. Enough to make it possible to breathe again. I wipe my nose on my sleeve and pull away, just enough to get a little bit of air between us, and look up at him.

His blue eyes, always so lively, have turned more intense and serious than I've ever seen them. His finger reaches up, traces one of the tear tracks on my cheek before brushing it away.

And before I have the chance to hold my breath, he's kissing the spot where the tear was. He turns toward my other cheek, pausing as his eyes linger on my bruise, and his shoulders go rigid. The touch of his lips, kissing my bruise, is so light it's hard to believe I'm not imagining it.

"Nick—" I say, my voice choked.

"Please don't cry," he whispers, resting his forehead against mine, his thumb stroking my cheek. "I'm sorry, I didn't mean to—"

And then the sound of someone clearing their throat jars us apart and my heart slams into my chest.

Dad.

Eight

Nick and I jerk apart as my father's glare turns icy, his hands twitching at his sides. For a second I think he'll yank Nick to his feet, but instead his chest just heaves and he stays there.

"Living room. *Now.*"

I scramble to my feet and walk briskly to the living room, feeling like a dog with its tail between its legs. I sniffle hard a few times, swiping at the tears that still threaten my eyes. I sit down in the corner of our wrap-around couch and Nick plunks down next to me. A milli-second later he leaps back to his feet, scoots down a full cushion, and sits again.

"Nothing happened," I say, gripping a throw pillow in my clenched hands.

"Don't lie to me, Samantha. I saw you two…" He clears his throat. "You know the rules. You're not allowed alone with boys. Nick is not to set foot in this house unless I'm here too." My dad is always ten times more intimidating in uniform, and right now he's pacing back and forth, his black laced-up boots thunking on the berber carpet. I've seen Nick eyeball the gun holstered on his hip at least three times.

"Dad. He's my best friend. It's not like that—"

"It sure as hell looked like it!"

"Sir—" Nick starts.

"And you!" he says, reeling on Nick. "What will your parents say when they hear of this?"

Nick stills. And then, in a low voice, says, "Not a whole lot. They *trust* me."

I know what he's implying, and I wait for my dad to pounce on him.

"I trust Sam!" he says, punctuating the air with his finger.

No, no he doesn't. He never has, and he never will. But I guess that's fair, because it's not like I trust him, either.

I hate when he does this… gets this air of authority, the whole "as long as you're under my roof" and "what I say goes" and "my way or the highway" all at once. It always manages to deflate me like I'm a balloon he's stepped on.

It's not like he hits me. Or cusses me out. If I tried to

tell people what he's like…they'd never understand. He's just…an intimidator. I don't know if it's his military background or being a cop or if it's just *him*.

"This isn't Sam's fault, sir. She was just upset—"

I shoot him a panicked look and he chokes on the rest of his sentence.

"Upset?" Dad asks, raising a brow. He gives Nick a long, lingering look. The sort he must use in interrogation. The sort that makes criminals confess. "What does she have to be upset about?

"She…"

"A girl at school vandalized my locker," I cut in.

Dad raises a brow. He wasn't expecting this. I've caught the Intimidator off-guard. He stands there and looks like he's chewing on something, but it's not like there's a toothpick sticking out his mouth so I have no idea what he's really doing. Chewing on the inside of his cheek?

"Sir, I promise you, nothing…happened," Nick cuts in. "She was just upset."

"That doesn't explain the two of you on the steps."

"I was giving her a hug."

His eyes narrow. For the first time, hope blooms. It's clear my dad didn't see the kiss. The sort-of kiss. It was only on the cheek, after all. Maybe if Dad had taken more than two seconds to look at us before exploding, he would have had a better view.

He turns and crosses his arms and stares us both down, somehow at the same time even though we're several feet apart. "You still broke the rules, Sam. I get your cell phone for a week." He holds out his hand. I open my mouth to argue, then snap it shut at the harshness in his eyes. Instead I just dig the phone out of my pocket and place it in his palm. "And Nick does not set foot inside this house unless I'm home, you got that?" he finishes.

I want to argue—I want to ask him what I'm being punished for in the first place—but I know better. Instead, I nod obediently. "Not a problem."

"And if I catch *anything* distasteful happening between the two of you, you'll be forbidden to see him at all. Do you understand?"

I nod. If they still made those chastity belt things, I'm sure my dad would make me wear one now, and then he'd wear the key around his neck. Why does he always assume the worst about me?

For the millionth time in my life, I wonder what would be happening right now if Mom still lived here. If she cared about me. If she would have been excited for me that my best friend might have more than platonic feelings … and they were mutual. If we would have had one of those embarrassing birds-and-bees conversations. If I would have confided things in her I could never tell my dad.

Fierce longing blooms in my chest but I shut it down. I always shut it down. She doesn't want me, so I shouldn't want her.

"Walk your *friend* to the door, Sam. I'm sure you have homework."

I nod and leap to my feet, eager for this entire embarrassment to be over. I follow Nick to the door and then step outside, holding the door partially shut.

"Sorry," I whisper.

"It's okay. I know your dad is … intense."

Intense. Sure, I guess that's a word for it. "You should go," I say.

Nick doesn't budge. "Turn your walkie-talkie on."

I can't help the curl at the edges of my lips. We haven't used those stupid things in … forever. We both got cell phones for our thirteenth birthdays and the walkie-talkies disappeared.

"Why?"

"We need to talk."

I swallow. In the freak-out with Dad, I nearly forgot what was really happening.

If he went postal over seeing a hug, I can't even imagine what would happen if he heard the rumors about Carter. He'd fly over to Carter's house with lights and sirens and probably break down the door with his shoulder, gun drawn.

I twist my hands together. "I won't talk about … you know."

It's funny that I can't say the words, when everyone else has no problem at all.

"You can't bottle it up. You're going to have to talk about it. Don't you get it? It's *criminal*, what he did. I can't believe you didn't report it."

I'm shaking my head, desperate for him to stop this line of thinking. "To who? My dad? Or the other cop in town?" I whisper. "I barely see daylight as it is. There's no way I'd tell him this." Funny how easy it is to go along with it, to avoid the truth. He'll know soon, but I can't do it like this, in rushed whispers on my front porch, hoping my dad won't hear. "Besides, don't you remember when we were kids, and we used to use the radios every night? People can listen in and it's just too…"

Much of a lie.

"Okay. But I don't like you being alone right now."

"Sam?"

My eyes flare as Dad's voice carries down the hall. I push Nick toward the steps, whispering, "Fine. Wait 'til eight, when my dad's shows start, and then I'll be on channel four."

He smiles, a soft smile, and for a heartbeat I forget everything else. "Talk then."

And then I'm left standing there, watching his retreat. Normally he'd just lope across the driveway with that odd, ungraceful run of his, but he has to move his car first. I'm surprised Dad didn't tell him he's broken at least three laws parking like that.

If I'd parked like that, he would have told me.

———

My palms are sweaty. Somehow that's all I can think, as I wipe them against my pink flannel pajama pants. It's 8:06 already, but it took me that long to quietly dig through the junk drawer in the kitchen and find a new nine-volt battery. We haven't used these things in so long, I forgot they even needed a battery.

Now, I click the dial on and then thumb through the channels until I get to channel four.

Static.

"You there?"

More static. Why do I feel so … fluttery? This is Nick. The same guy I whupped at Wii last weekend. The same guy I tease and joke with.

But it's not just the same guy I've always known. It's also the guy who kissed me on Sunday. Three times. The guy who held my hand in the halls this morning. The same guy who wiped away my tears and kissed my cheek.

"About time," comes the loud response. I jump and scramble to turn down the volume.

I click the button on the side and hold the mic up to my mouth. "Sorry. I forgot these things took nine-volt batteries. I had to raid the junk drawer. Dad had spares, of course, for the smoke detectors."

I click it off and wait for his response, pulling the covers over my shoulders.

"Your dad is more prepared than a Boy Scout."

I laugh and then realize I wasn't holding the button. It's funny, how different these are than our cells. I click the button down. "Don't I know it."

"You sure you're okay? He really flipped out on us."

I lean back against my pillow and stare at the shadows in the corner of my room. Am I? Right now … yes. It's the first time all day I haven't thought about … the things raging at school. "Yeah."

"Really? I just feel … terrible. We were together all weekend and I had no idea—

"I don't really want to talk about it. Not right now … on the radios."

"Okay."

I click the button a few times but I can't figure out what to say so I just let it go.

"What?" he says, his voice crackling.

I sit up in my bed and part the blinds with my thumb and pointer finger, just a couple of inches so I can peer out into the burgeoning darkness.

"Open your drapes," I say.

They flutter for a second and then there he is, sitting in his bed, his elbow propped up on the windowsill. All at once I'm ten again and we're talking about that half-assed fort we spent a year building in the woods behind his backyard. The worries at school seem to fade as I stare across at him.

"This is kind of fun." I release the button and let the walkie-talkie fall into my lap, then reach to pull up my blinds so there's a two-foot gap above the sill. Now I can see him without holding the blinds in one hand.

"It kind of reminds me of Legos," he says.

I laugh. "Why?"

I watch as he raises the walkie to his mouth, blocking his lips. It's weird, watching him and not seeing him speak but hearing his voice crackle across the walkie. "Because that's all I did the summer I got the walkies. Play Legos."

"I was thinking about our fort."

I watch his shoulders shake and then he shakes his head. "I'm surprised neither of us plummeted to our deaths. Carpenters, we are not."

"Oh come on, it wasn't that bad," I say, indignant.

"Are you kidding? We thought we could use staples to secure a two-by-four to the trees." He holds the walkie-talkie away from his face and raises his brows, the cutest little smirk on his lips. I can just make it out in the shadows, the warm yellow light of his room spilling out into the darkness around him.

I pretend to act outraged. I'm glad it's nearly summer, or it would be too dark to make out his expression. "We figured out that wouldn't work," I say.

"Eventually."

I can't help it. I grin. It's weird how we're so far apart, the expanse of grass between our houses separating us, and yet I can see the bright blue of his eyes, as if they're reflecting the gleam of the stars and the moon overhead. They're boring right into me. Seeing me in a way I'm not sure they ever have. I lean forward until my nose is nearly touching the screen. Then I click the button again. "As the girl, I was supposed to be your assistant. As the guy, you were supposed to be the carpenter."

"Right. Well, by that theory, those cookies we made were entirely your fault."

I scoff. Then click on my walkie. "In my defense, your

mother told us baking soda and baking powder were the same thing."

"Hey, at least *my* mom tries to help!"

My grin fades, and a half-beat later, so does Nick's. "God I'm sorry, that came out wrong."

I shrug and purse my lips. Nick raises the walkie to his lips again. "Your dad loves you, you know, or he wouldn't have freaked on us like that."

I shake my head. "No, he loved my mom. And ... " I sigh. "Let's talk about something else."

We stare across at one another, our radios silent, the sounds of crickets filling the void.

I watch him raise the radio to his lips. "Pickles."

A laugh bursts forth, catching me off guard. "Pickles?"

"Yes. I'm partial to the sweet and crunchy ones, myself. Spears, preferably."

I roll my eyes but I'm grinning again. "You're so weird sometimes."

"That's why you love me," he says.

I never noticed before how much he says that. Maybe because I now think it might be true. Does he know this, somehow? Is that why he says it?

I ignore the lingering look he gives me, forcing our conversation to stay light. "Yep. It's that and your old Seattle Sonics T-shirt. Armpit holes get me every time." I put a hand to my chest as if to still my fluttery heart, and he scoffs at me. Then I'm smiling again.

Nick tips his head to the side, giving me a serious look, and my grin fades. I know he thinks I shouldn't be smiling like this, or maybe he thinks I'm using it to cover up my darker issues. Darker issues that don't actually exist. "You really do need to tell your dad what happened," he says.

"I told you, I really don't want to talk about it."

"He's the chief of police, Sam. He'll know what to do."

"Last I checked, he didn't own a time machine, so there's nothing he can do to fix it or change it. Just drop it, Nick."

He sighs. I don't hear it, but I can see his shoulders heave.

"I should go to bed before Dad wonders what's going on up here and checks on me."

Nick nods. "Okay. G'night, Sam."

I lower the blinds and fall back against my bed again. "Good night, Nick."

And then before I can click it off, he says one last thing: "Sweet dreams."

But to dream, I have to sleep, and that's going to be impossible. I climb under my blankets and stare at the sliver of light coming in through the windows.

I wish there really was a way to reverse time—to go back to the party and stay out of Carter's bedroom. I wish I could spend that evening with Nick, playing pool.

It was stupid, to try and use Carter to get Nick's attention.

I punch my pillow a few times, reshaping it until I can tuck it comfortably up under my arm. I close my eyes, but my body still hums with energy.

It's going to be a long night.

Nine

Three hours later I give up, sliding a blank notebook out from under my bed and grabbing a pen from my nightstand. I click on my little white lamp, then prop myself up on pillows.

I've written at least a dozen novels in the last three years. Fun, dorky novels. They're nothing like real life, just total escapism, the literary equivalent of a rom-com. Since they're in the trash now, it's time to write something else.

Something real.

My pen hits the paper, makes the comforting, scratchy noise that always seems to soothe me.

But after I write the words *Chapter One*, all I do is

stare at the lines on the paper until they blur together and my eyes feel like sandpaper and two hours have passed.

Nothing. That's what I write. When the alarm goes off, I discover I've drifted to sleep on a blank page.

When I look myself in the mirror the next morning, I have dark circles under my bloodshot eyes.

I just keep thinking about how Carter must feel right now, with this rumor floating around him. Maybe he laughed it off. Maybe people don't really believe it.

Please let people not really believe it.

But Nick does. Because I cried and now he believes me, and he shouldn't, and God I feel heavy right now, the weight of everything pressing down on me.

I want desperately to call in sick to school. Wallow in bed and ignore the storm that's raging inside those halls. But my dad will notice my car sitting in the driveway because he makes a point of patrolling our house when he's out and about, as if anyone is crazy enough to break into the police chief's house.

So I walk away from the mirror that's taunting me with my haggard reflection and instead I take a shower, dawdling under the hot steam until the water heater, predictably, gives up and nothing but cold water sputters out. Then I get dressed, brushing my hair free of tangles as I stare at my ugly reflection in the mirror.

I descend the steps, my socks silent on the carpet, and

go to the kitchen to get an apple and grab my car keys. My dad is at the counter, pouring coffee into the stainless steel thermos he keeps in his cruiser all day. If I thought I could get away with it, I'd whirl around and bolt, but my keys are hanging on the hook right behind him.

"Morning," I say, walking past him.

"Morning." He puts the empty pot in the sink and glances over his shoulder at me. "Your cell phone is on the table," he says, his voice oddly remorseful.

I stop, blinking. Why is my dad waving a white flag? "I thought you were taking it for a week."

"You can have it back. But the other rules, about Nick, still stand."

I narrow my eyes. "So I'm not in trouble, but my best friend still isn't allowed over?"

"I know you think I make up these rules to torture you, but it's for your own good."

"How is banning Nick from the house unless you're around good for me?"

I never argue like this, and as soon as the words are out, I want to reel them back in.

He turns around and gives me a glare cold enough to freeze the Bahamas. "Do not argue with me or you *will* lose your phone," he says. "Now, are you going to tell me why you were upset yesterday? And do I need to talk to your principal about your locker?"

Panic seizes my chest. "Dad, I can't tell you—we don't have that kind of relationship. And I don't need you going to school like you're going to fix things. It wasn't a big deal. They've probably fixed my locker anyway." I hope.

"What do you mean, *that kind* of relationship?"

It's all I can do not to roll my eyes. "You know, the heart-to-heart kind."

"You can talk to me," he says.

"Can I? Really?"

"Of course," he says, twisting the top on his thermos.

He's delusional. He doesn't even know he's delusional. "Whatever," I say, heading to the door.

"Sam, I mean it. I'm your father. If you need me to talk to the principal ... "

"No, I told you, I got it," I say.

Two more months and I can escape to UW. *Two more months.*

I throw on some ballet flats and head out to my car without saying goodbye.

I start it up and pull away, but for a long while I can't force myself to go to school. I end up circling the residential streets for ten minutes straight, until I know I'm pushing it and I'll get marked tardy if I don't give in.

Finally, I turn right like I'm supposed to, and the school looms in the distance. I feel sick. Weak, and a little dizzy. I can't seem to do anything but park as if on autopilot, taking note of the way a girl walking by me elbows her friend, nods in my direction.

Today, I have to undo this. Rewind time and make people understand the truth of the situation, and not the lie they so easily believed.

Something shifted yesterday, with Nick and me, when I broke down crying. How am I going to tell him I was crying because of what was happening to me at school, and not because Carter actually did it?

All I want to do is pretend nothing is wrong and avoid it all, for eternity, but I know I can't. I need to face Nick, tell him the truth, and ask if he'll help me. He's the freakin' class president, the one with all the power. He can set this right.

Then I'll fake a stomachache and go to the nurses to lie down. The whole thing will blow over. Disappear. By my last class, it'll be like it didn't even happen. Other than the ugly word on my locker, which by now, I pray, has been fixed.

It's only a matter of time.

I hold my backpack in front of my chest with both arms, like it's a Kevlar vest. But words are more deadly than bullets. Even if they're the words you didn't say and not the ones you did.

I go to my locker, avoiding looking at anyone. The marker is gone, and a fresh coat of paint gleams back at me. Relief swoops through me. I quickly spin the lock, popping the door open in seconds. A scrap of paper flutters to my feet. Weird.

I scoop up the torn paper and flip it over.

Tell the truth. Now. Or you will regret it.

It's not the same writing as on the locker. It's smaller, slanted.

Carter wrote it himself. My hand shaking, I shove the

paper into my pocket. As I grab my English textbook, a hand grasps my arm. My heart leaps into my throat and I whirl around.

Nick. He loosens his grip a bit when he sees my expression. "I was going to pick you up this morning, but you were already gone."

I tap on the Diet Coke can in my hand. "Needed my fix so I stopped by a gas station." Another lie, to go with all the others.

"Oh." He lets go of my arm. I'm not sure what he's thinking—that I need a personal body guard? He never gives me a ride to school, since he always stays after for all his activities.

His eyes sweep over me, like he needs to make sure I'm still in one piece.

"I'm not going to explode at any moment, you know," I say, squaring my shoulders and hoping he buys it. I don't know, I could actually explode.

He leans in so closely his lips are brushing my skin, his breath hot on my ear. "Sorry, I just don't know how to act right now. I'm worried about you."

I pull back. "How about normal?" I give him a look like he's being ridiculous, but maybe he's not. What if Carter *had* raped me? Would I need someone to pick me up, hold me together?

Would I even go to school today?

Nick glances around at everyone staring at us. My bravado deflates like a car tire with a nail in it. There's nothing normal about this situation. And my cavalier attitude isn't selling anyone.

I have to tell him, but I can't tell him here. Not now. He'll freak out on me, just like he was freaking out yesterday, and things will just end up worse. I need to figure out exactly what I plan to say, and then talk to him in private, where he can't run off before I'm done fully explaining.

I'll tell him tonight, at home. I'll explain why it happened, how it all spiraled out of control. It's not like I did this on purpose. Jeez, at the same time I finally figured out what was going on, someone was already writing *whore* on my locker. Why would I want any of this?

He'll understand. He'll help me.

"Normal. Okay," he says. "How about I walk with you to class. Does that fit the definition?"

"Sure."

But when he turns toward the row of classroom doors, he takes my hand in his, and his fingers interlace with mine. Holding hands with my best friend is not normal. It's … new. I feel the heat of him next to me, want to lean into him.

When he squeezes my hand, he smiles tentatively at me, a smile that lingers so long it's like I'm basking in it, soaking it in and letting it erase the world around me, until it's just me and him.

"Nice to see your dad didn't lock you up for all eternity," he says.

"He'd love to. If he thought for a second he could do it and get away with it, he probably would."

We make it to the door of our English class, and just as we're about to go in, he stops me. "You sure you can handle this today? I can—"

I put a finger up to his lips to silence him. I would have done it without a second thought a few days ago, but now all I can feel is his lips, warm and soft against my finger. I want him to kiss me again, like he did in the dog-wash room, like in his car. I blink and try to remember what I'd planned to say. "It's okay. I'm not going to fall into a million pieces."

I seem to hate myself more with each thing I say to him. Each thing that seems to imply I really *am* grappling with the repercussions of rape. Each thing I say that tells him I'm plagued by something darker than I can even comprehend.

I can tell myself *I didn't lie* a hundred times, but I know what I'm doing now. I know what they all think.

He leans forward, brushing his lips against mine, just for a millisecond. I can feel my blood in my veins, thicker than molasses; it's as if I can hear my heartbeat thumping in my chest, slower with each beat.

Nick smiles, leads me into the classroom, and we plunk into our seats beside one another just as a shrill bell rings out.

I hope I don't lose him when he finds out the truth.

Ten

I have a smashed bag of chips buried in the bottom of my backpack, so I swing by the cafeteria just long enough to grab a soda before scurrying off to the library. Nick's going to look for me at lunch, I know he will, and that's why I keep my eyes down, not daring to look at anyone, my hood pulled up around my hair.

I'm not ready to tell him yet, and I don't want to tell him at school, so I just need some time alone.

I'm crossing the courtyard, nearly to the library, when a hand reaches out and I whirl around, slamming straight into the hard chest of a guy at least a foot taller than me. The air is knocked from my lungs but the guy hardly flinches at the way I careened right into him. When I meet his gaze, my insides seem to shrink away.

Brent. He moved to Mossyrock in sixth grade. He lives a block from Carter's house and he's on the football team. I step away, but I just knock into someone else. I whirl around but only manage to turn halfway, since Brent hasn't released my arm. And then suddenly he does, but just so he can push me into the other guy, Anton, who promptly pushes right back. Just like that, I'm a pinball.

"We want to know when we get our turn," Anton says, his voice a calm, seductive drawl. My skin crawls. "Word has it you give it up willingly."

I blink furiously, trying to rip my arm from his grasp. What is he saying? Are there *other* rumors?

No, they're on Carter's side. They don't believe the rumors, that's what they mean. They're telling me it didn't happen.

The false seduction drops and he glares at me, hard. "This is your warning. Undo it now."

And all at once, they're both gone and I'm left standing there, shivering in the seventy-degree sunshine. I whirl around and all but run to the library, my hood falling off of my head and my hair streaming behind me.

When I finally make it inside, I nearly slam the door shut. The utter silence of the library greets me, at odds with the loud *thunk* of the door against the jamb. A set of narrowed eyes stare at me from the librarian's desk. She raises a finger to her lips and keeps glaring. I cringe and shrink away, weaving between the tall shelves of the reference section. I find a quiet couch in the back and sink down, dropping my backpack and willing my heart to slow.

I kick my ballet flats off and curl my legs up underneath me, reaching down to unzip my backpack and pull out my binder. Maybe if I pretend to be busy, no one will bother me.

My theory lasts for a mere minute and a half, because before I know what's happening, Michelle Pattison is sitting down at the other end of the couch, all awkward smiles and sheepish looks.

Michelle Pattison is the bane of my existence. What does she think she's doing, sitting down like that? That she's allowed to spread the most grossly negligent rumor in the history of the universe and it's all going to be okay? That I'd be willing to give her the time of day after what she started?

If she hadn't seen me walk out of Carter's room, if she hadn't asked those stupid questions I'm not entirely sure I answered, this wouldn't have happened.

"Hey," she says, sinking deeper into the couch. This couch needs to be replaced. It's like it's trying to eat students alive, pull them right in so they can't get out.

"Hi." I barely glance upward. I dig a pencil out and start filling in random notes on an old page of English homework.

I hope she'll get the point, but she doesn't seem to. I'm so screwed.

"Are you doing okay? I mean, you looked so shook up at Carter's," she says, leaning in. I want to believe she's being genuine and helpful or something, but I know the truth. She wants more gossip.

"Yep. Life is glorious," I say, hoping she catches my sarcasm.

"I feel *so bad* about what happened to you, you know? You must be going through total hell right now," she says.

Yeah. Something like that. I clear my throat, try not to meet her eyes. "Well, you know. Uh, I'm ... handling it."

I lean in closer to my homework, narrowing my eyes like I'm trying really, really hard to concentrate.

"Look, this is a little awkward, but I got you something."

And then she shoves something in front of me, on top of the homework I've been so intently staring at.

"I went to the counselor and got some information for you. I thought maybe ... " Her voice trails off as she waves the pamphlet under my nose.

My face burns as red-hot shame courses through me. I snatch the pamphlet and shove it into my binder as the words *Assistance for Victims of Sexual Assault* register.

This cannot be happening. I cannot be discussing this with her. My head suddenly feels heavy, my throat thick. They really believe it. They really think Carter went too far in his bedroom last Friday. They really think I'm a victim, broken by Carter.

They really think he's capable of that.

"Thanks, Michelle. That was, uh, nice of you."

"Do you want to go with me to the counselor?" Michelle asks, her voice soft. "She's super sweet, and I promise she'll listen to you without judging. Sometimes I go just to talk about my mom and dad splitting up. Oh God, not that that's, like, the same thing as rape or anything."

I swallow. "Uh, I just really need to work on my English homework, you know?"

She wrinkles her nose, stares right at me, and in that moment I have this dreadful feeling that she *knows* and is about to call me on it. "I thought those term papers were the last homework. I'm not missing something, am I? It would be just like Mr. Grant to assign something at the last minute when half the students are already outside the door."

"Uh, no, I mean, it's … extra credit."

"Oh." This answer seems to only sort of pacify her and she looks as if she's about to question it, but then she snaps her mouth shut.

"I hope you know, if you ever need me, for anything, I am so there for you. I mean, to think I was the first person there … I wish I had known what was happening and done something for you, you know? I'm just … really sorry. I can't stop thinking about it and feeling guilty."

If she doesn't leave in, like, the next five seconds, I think I might totally scream at her. I want to blame her for all this, want to unleash the wave of guilt building inside me, direct it all at her. I want her to rewind it all, unsay the things she said, undo the things I've done.

It's not her fault, but I want it to be.

"Anyway, I have to get to lunch before Katie misses me, but seriously, let me know if you need me, okay?"

Yes, I got that. If not the first and second time, the third. "Sure. I just want to be left alone now, okay?"

"Alright, well, have a good day, okay? Or I mean, as good as it could be, considering."

"Bye, Michelle."

She finally gets the hint. I watch her walk away, feeling my opportunity slip through my grasp as the door closes. Her words started this, and maybe they could have ended it. But I couldn't seem to say it.

I wonder if she was being sincere this whole time, not just rooting for gossip. Maybe I have her all wrong. Maybe she was really wanting to help me. If I even needed that kind of help.

She and her little friends probably sat around and discussed the idea of her going to the counselor, getting me a brochure. They probably all wondered how I'm dealing with being raped, thinking I need a support system. She's probably scurrying off to the cafeteria right now to tell them how it all went.

My cheeks burn again. They're all picturing what happened, thinking of me in Carter's room ... him on top of me ...

I sigh and sink against the couch. It's weird, how this is becoming one big train wreck and yet I just keep watching it, unable to find the guts to just blurt out the truth. Why do I keep doing this?

I can't let go of the control on this. I need to be able to decide how they all find out. I need everyone to know that I never *said* he did it.

And somehow I have to do it without losing Nick.

Eleven

Apparently, it only takes a day to master staring straight ahead. I navigate the halls with blinders, pretending I don't see the curious looks, the smirks, the pity.

I hate the pity. They should hate me, not feel sorry for me.

"Sam!" I hear my voice being called, and I glance back as I walk, trying to figure out where it came from. "Sam, stop!"

I twist back around to see where I'm going, and then stumble to a stop.

I'm standing face to face with Carter.

We're both so shocked we don't move for a second, but

then I take a large step back, away from him, as my heart takes flight in my chest and my hands tremble as they grasp my textbook.

"You little—"

"Sam!" Veronica is next to me now, grabbing my arm, pulling me away from Carter. He steps forward. "Who the hell do you think you are?" he asks, his voice rising. "You fucking—"

"Carter!" someone barks, a deep, authoritative voice. "What do you think—"

"She's a fucking liar is what I think!" Carter yells, and I twist around to see Mr. Trenton, a science teacher I've had for three years straight. He's looking over my head, glaring at Carter.

"Mr. Wellesley!" he roars. "You're headed straight to the principal's—"

"*I'm* going to the office? When *she's*—"

"Let's get out of here," Veronica whispers into my ear. "Now."

I can't speak because I can barely breathe as the panic takes over everything and the flight instinct finally kicks in.

Carter's distracted by Mr. Trenton just long enough for me to round a corner and lose sight of him.

"That was close," Veronica says. "I can't *believe* he'd go after you here. After what he did! Is he totally delusional?"

I just nod. I think my knees are going to give out. Veronica steers me to a bench outside, next to a big rhododendron.

"Okay, just sit down, take a couple of deep breaths.

God, you are so ashen right now. Do you want to go to the nurse?"

The nurse's office is next door to the principal. "No, I'll be okay."

"You sure? You're shaking."

I look down at my hands, which are still trembling, still tightly gripping my books. "Just give me a minute," I croak out.

"Okay. God, that was intense. I tried to warn you but you were halfway down the hall. I can't believe he'd do that. He cussed you out right in front of a teacher!"

I take in the deepest breath I can manage and start to feel my heartbeat come back under control, feel the blood come back into my limbs.

"Maybe you should report him," she says. "You could probably get a restraining order—"

"I don't want to talk about it right now," I say. "Please, let's not talk about it."

My voice comes out harsher than I'd meant it to, and Veronica snaps her jaw shut.

"I'm sorry. I'm just…I'm stressed out right now and I don't want to think about it."

"Okay. Not a problem."

We sit outside until the bell rings and we're officially late, and then I get up and follow her back through the doors, into the now-empty halls.

———

When I get home that afternoon, my plate of dinner is already waiting for me in the microwave. Some kind of gross-looking lasagne, from a frozen box no doubt. But my dad will explode if I don't eat it because he thinks I look too skinny as it is, so I nuke it for so long it'll just burn off my taste buds and I won't have to know what it tastes like. It's all goopy and steaming when I pull it out. I cover it in salt and pepper and a little shredded cheese, hoping that will make it easier to get down.

I wonder if I'll learn how to cook, if I get to college. Or if it'll be more frozen dinners.

If. I just said *if.* Why am I thinking of it like that? It's *when* I get to college.

Isn't it? I already sent in the paperwork. The deposits. I'm eighteen, so I didn't need Dad's permission.

Legally, that is.

I take it to the kitchen table because "we don't eat in front of the television in this house," unless you're Dad, that is, and one of his precious games is on. Then he forgets to put a coaster under his root beer, and he dribbles hot wings sauce on his jersey, and I avoid the living room.

I use the fork in my left hand and a pen in my right, and I open the same blank notebook to the first page, still pristine and unmarked, and stare at the place where I wrote *Chapter One.*

I'm still sitting there an hour later, doodling absent-mindedly in the margins of an otherwise blank page, my empty plate beside me, when Dad walks in.

Dang. I thought he was on swing shift or something.

Most of the time, he's gone twelve or fourteen hours a day, even though I know his shift doesn't last that long.

"Feet off the table," he says, going to the fridge. I roll my eyes while his back is turned and put my feet down, resting my heels on the bar underneath my chair.

"What time does the graduation ceremony start?"

I keep drawing circles on the notepad, filling them in with dark blue. "It's not until this weekend."

"That's not what I asked," he says.

I chew on the inside of my cheek. "Four, I think."

"You think or you know?"

I clench my teeth. "The invite is on the fridge three inches from your face. Why don't you just read it?"

He whirls around. I can't believe I just said that.

"Don't sass me," he says.

"Or what?" I lean back, feeling oddly defiant.

He grips the handle to the fridge even harder. "Or I'll choose your fall quarter classes *for* you."

I snort. He's not choosing my classes. He's not even choosing my college. He only thinks he is.

"Something funny?"

I cross my arms. "When are you going to give up control, Dad? When I'm thirty?"

"If you're lucky," he says, turning back to the fridge.

I open my mouth. I want to tell him. I *need* to tell him. I think of the paperwork sitting upstairs. The classes I've already registered for, *thank you very much*. Part of me fantasizes about just … packing up and leaving nothing but a note. He can figure it out.

But I don't say anything. I just snap my jaw shut, push my chair back, and stomp off to my room, wondering if I'll actually follow through with it.

I glance across the yard at Nick's window. I need him to get home, immediately. What is taking so long? I need to tell him what I wasn't able to tell Michelle. What I haven't been able to tell anyone.

He left his drapes open, and I can see his computer desk and a big poster of Earth on the wall above his rumpled-up, unmade bed. That's so like comfortable, casual Nick. He probably doesn't even notice. He probably rolls out of bed, throws on some random clothes and a ball cap, and strolls to school to be admired.

My dad would flip if I left my room a mess like that. I'd be grounded for a week. Sometimes I think my dad runs around just looking and hoping for reasons to ground me, to keep me penned up under this roof forever and ever. He wants me to be the princess in the tower, locked away for eternity, pining for a prince who will never arrive.

Nick has no idea how many times I fantasized that his window was mine, that his parents were mine. Imagined myself walking into his house, plunking down at the counter, and telling his mom about my day. She'd smile and laugh and fix me a snack and make it all go away.

He must have some idea, though. We hardly hang out at my house at all. I always find reasons for us to leave. If it weren't for my dad, it would be kinda of silly, because our houses are exactly the same. The floor plans are simply reversed, so that their garage is on the right and ours is on the left. Our bedrooms are laid out like someone put a mirror between them, making a perfect reflection: a large closet along the same wall as the entry door, and two tall windows, one near each of our beds. And yet his room always feels like bliss, like a sanctuary, and mine feels more like a prison.

My dad loves Nick's parents, and he thinks we spend the whole time in the kitchen or the living room, under adult supervision. If he knew his parents weren't the type to watch us like hawks, he probably wouldn't let me visit Nick over there, either.

Today, Nick doesn't come over to my house. At five, after I know his student council meeting is over, I sit on the edge of my bed and just stare at his window. So close, yet so far away. My heart pounds harder with each passing minute. It was easier to imagine telling him when it was hours away, but now, it seems nearly impossible to think of sitting in front of him and telling him that the truth I made him believe about Carter wasn't *truth* at all.

Finally, the rumbling of his Mustang sounds in the distance, growing louder as he glides down the road, pulls into his driveway. All I can see through the tinted window are his hands gripping the wheel. He doesn't move for a long moment and I want to know what his expression is. He never sits in his car like that. He bounds out with that off-kilter gait of his, across the lawn, and up the steps to his house. I imagine he's scowling, upset about what he thinks happened to me.

I really have to go over there and confess it all.

Just the thought of it sends my insides into a flurry of knots.

Finally, his hands disappear, the driver's side door swings open, and he's standing. He shields his eyes from the spring sun and looks right at me. I just lean on my elbow and meet his gaze. He lifts his eyebrows toward his bedroom and then wiggles his finger. I nod and disappear back into my room, to throw on my slippers and scramble down the steps.

I have to tell him. *I will tell him.* Now. Immediately.

I slip outside and in hardly a second, I'm standing in front of him.

Nick stands there, chewing on his lip, blinking, staring back at me for a long stretch of a moment. "You still doing okay?"

I nod.

"Want to watch a movie?"

I nod again. He slings an arm loosely around my shoulders and guides me over to their cedar porch, all the cute little geraniums pots just beginning to bloom. Our porch is desolate and empty, like the rest of the house. I have the sudden urge to steal a pot and bring it to my house.

It would die, if I did.

Inside, we kick off our shoes and he pulls me up the stairs. I try not to fixate on every spot where our skin touches, every time our arms or hips bump, but it's impossible. Three kisses, and it's like we were never just friends. It's like we've always been what I wanted us to be. But does it matter? I have to tell him the truth about Carter, and what if he doesn't forgive me?

Maybe it's too late. Maybe it's unforgiveable. My heart lurches. I don't know if I could handle that. I need Nick to understand that I'm not a bad person, that I didn't run out and create this lie.

We make it up to his room, and he clicks the door shut—his parents never made any rules about girls coming over because Nick's too perfect in their eyes; he can do no wrong. As soon as it's closed, Nick spins around, enveloping me in a hug, holding me against his chest.

"Are you *really* doing okay? I'm worried about you. It's like you're pretending it didn't happen or something. Faking normal and hoping it's true."

That same haunting guilt sears through me.

No, I'm not doing okay. And no, it's not what you think it is.

I clench my jaw and swallow, wishing I could just tell him right now, with him holding me up against him, when I can't see his eyes. But I just breathe deeply and remember the smell of him this close, close my eyes and feel the comforting weight of his arms around me, and I'm scared. Terrified.

I'm scared of losing this before I ever really had it. I'm scared that after months and months of pining for him, he could turn his back on me, go away to Yale, and never look back.

I'm scared of losing the only person who has ever been there for me. And so all I do is nod and try to memorize exactly how this feels, because I know without a doubt he'll leave me.

He kisses the top of my head and then slips his arms from my shoulders. He goes to the TV and flips through his stack of DVDs, holding two out. "Comedy or drama?"

"Comedy." Something stupid and mindless is exactly what I need. I perch on the edge of the bed and pick a few pieces of lint off of his suede bedspread. My toes bury themselves into the deep-pile, cream-colored area rug at the foot of the bed. I stare at Nick's backside as he steps backward, a remote in hand and aimed at the DVD player. The screen pops up and he clicks "play." I expect him to sit down next to me, but he goes to the door first and flips off the light switch. My stomach lurches.

It's still bright in the room, so Nick slides the drapes shut, and my stomach lunges again. Have we watched movies in the dark before? All of the sudden I can't remember. I want the answer to be no.

When he sits down next to me, it's all I can do to keep my eyes on the screen and not the tiny shred of space between our thighs, just a tiny little patch of green quilt. My muscles tense and I want to close that distance, feel the heat of his body through my jeans.

I'm sitting on the edge of the bed, my legs hanging down, my back stiff as a board. When Nick scoots back to prop himself up on the pillows, I go rigid, stay frozen at the edge of the bed.

"Uh, are you going to sit like that through the whole movie? Your big head is kind of blocking the TV."

Half my nerves flood out at Nick's words. So like our normal conversations. So ... *Nick*. Something hits me and I turn around to see his goofy half-smile. I pick up the pillow and roll my eyes. "No."

I scoot back until I'm propped up on at least three pillows. How have I never noticed how small this bed is? How our knees and elbows touch?

I shift around, trying to get comfortable, wanting to scoot closer to him and further away at the same time. Is it just me or is he leaning slightly toward me?

God, I'm losing it. Why is it a big deal if *Nick* leans toward me? This isn't a freakin' date.

Is it?

I blink several times and stare at the poster that hangs over the top of the TV. The same poster I've seen a thousand times before. This is *Nick*. Why am I freaking out like this? He's my best friend. I've seen him go skinny dipping. Okay, so I covered my eyes mostly, but I saw skin. He tried to convince me to go too but I chickened out, just like I'm sure he expected me to.

Now I wish I hadn't chickened out.

Our arms are definitely touching now. The hairs on mine stand up. I breathe as normally as possible but I swear my lungs aren't quite filling up.

"I'm sorry I freaked out on you yesterday," he says.

I wave my hand. "Water under the bridge," I say.

Now. I should tell him *right now* what really happened. "No, you didn't deserve that. I just ... panicked. And I made you cry. And with what you're dealing with, you need someone to be there, not yell at you. I just feel so guilty ... "

"It wasn't you. It was my whole day. I was so confused when I got to school ... " I take in a deep breath. I need to just lay it all out there. "People were staring and I didn't understand why, what they were all talking about, and then I overheard these girls in the bathroom and realized everyone was saying Carter ... " My voice breaks and I can't seem to say the words. I don't think I ever *have* said them, which I suppose is the ironic part, right? That I can't even say the words and everyone else has no problem?

I feel smothered by it all. Smashed and weighted down by the lie. Half of me wants to tell the truth and end it all, but the other half wants to keep it going, act as though nothing is wrong at all. I'm eaten up inside.

I sit up in bed and chew harder on my lip. "I never meant for any of this to happen. I mean, it's not like I went out and told people he did that. You know that, right?"

Nick sits up next to me, takes my chin between his thumb and finger, and turns me to look at him, his eyes boring into me. For a long second, I wonder if he can see the truth in my eyes. I half expect him to jerk away and call me a liar. "Of course I know that. No one ever wants something like this to happen."

I groan inwardly, breaking our eye contact and looking down at my fingers as I twist and wrench them together. He's not understanding what I'm trying to say. What I *need* to say.

Nick clears his throat, twisting a few strands of my

hair between his fingers, and I close my eyes and memo-rize the feel of it. We're so close, our skin inches apart. What if I tell him, and I never feel it again? What if he's disgusted by me?

"I need to tell you something," Nick says.

"Me too," I blurt. Panic and fear swell immediately. "I mean, uh, you. You can go first."

He lets go of a long sigh, drops his hand so that he's not touching me any more. "Reyna gave me an ultimatum."

I blink. I was not expecting that. "Huh?"

"Before we broke up. She said it was her or you."

"You told me she didn't like you talking about me so much."

"Well, it was more than that. She could tell I wanted to be more than friends with you. She said I had to stop seeing either you or her, because she wasn't going to play second best."

My jaw no longer seems to work. I'm just staring at him, lips parted. Even Reyna knew he liked me? How could she see it when I didn't?

"It's funny, really," he says.

"What is?"

"That she noticed it before I did. How strongly I felt about you. I mean, I knew, I guess, but I was afraid to ruin our friendship. I was afraid you didn't feel that way. So I was trying to talk myself out of it. But she could see through it."

His fingers stop stroking my skin. "And now I hate myself because I should have acted on it a month ago, when we broke up. When I realized she was right. I could have been there for you on Friday—I could have stopped that from happening. But I was too busy sulking in the game room, picturing you with Carter."

He smiles a soft, sad smile. "I'm going to hate myself forever for that, you know? I should have protected you."

The silence hangs over us like a too-heavy veil, and I'm suffocated by it.

He feels guilty. That he didn't stop something that didn't happen.

My stomach is like a bowling ball, heavy and uncomfortable, and I shift around on the bed, but it doesn't go away. I have to tell Nick the truth. I have to.

He clears his throat. "Anyway, what did you want to say?"

"Huh?"

"You said you had something to confess too."

I blink. "Oh."

My lips tremble as I try to force the words out through the wedge in my throat. What if I lose him before I ever really had him?

I can't. I can't lose him, not now. He's the only one in my life who has ever really mattered.

"Uh, I forgot."

"Oh."

Tomorrow. I'll tell him tomorrow.

Twelve

After the movie, I'm back at home, curled up in my chair with the same blank notebook, feeling lower than ever. I've put it off for another day. How *could* I have told him, though? When he chose me over beautiful, exotic Reyna?

I could never be what she is: pretty and outgoing. I'm always going to be stuck in this too-skinny body with too-frizzy curls and too-narrow eyes. I don't deserve him. Our friendship is strong; it could survive a lot. But I don't know if it could survive this. Nick would never let me ruin Carter like I am and then just ... forgive me.

Maybe I shouldn't tell him. Maybe I shouldn't tell *anyone*.

I close my eyes and heave a deep breath. Of *course* I will tell the truth.

I pick up a pen and lean forward, staring at the doodles and blank lines on the pages of the notebook.

Words used to come easily to me. Even before I knew I wanted to be a writer for a living, I was already a writer. The words would flow the second I put the pen on the paper.

But tonight...

Nothing happens. I'm empty of words, of stories, of anything. I'm as empty as the page in front of me. I groan and throw the pen across the room. How can I be a professional writer when... I can't seem to write?

I click on my Facebook bookmark, glancing up at the calendar pinned over my desk. Four days until graduation. Four days until I tell my dad where I'm going to college.

When I look back at the screen, I can't help but recoil, sit way back in my chair. My whole page is filled with messages, and a bubble tells me I have seven private messages, too.

Tracey: *Hugs*. Hope you're okay.

Vic: You're a fucking liar.

Vic is Carter's co-captain for the basketball team. I hit the X and delete his comment.

Britney: OMG!! I know we haven't talked forever but I
hope you're okay!

Mindy: My thoughts are with you...

The glory of living in a town with a graduating class of
forty-five. We all know each other, and Facebook is pretty
much auto-friending. The cheerleaders don't talk to me,
but they don't mind sending me friend requests.

Brent: I meant what I said.

The guy who grabbed me in the courtyard. Carter's
best friend. My stomach clenches as I delete his comment. He wasn't in the room. He doesn't know what
really happened.

But he's right.

I start deleting them all, without reading them. Half
the school wants to give me virtual hugs and the other half
wants to bash me, and none of them are my friends anyway. Most of these people haven't spoken two words to me
in months, unless it was some part of a school assignment.

The only one who *is* my friend is the one whose window stares right at mine—but it doesn't matter, because
the truth will tear us apart.

I open my private message box and start deleting
those, too. But then I see one I am afraid to click on.

Who the hell do you think you are? is the subject line. And
it's from Carter. It arrived this morning.

My mouse hovers over the X. I should just delete it.

There is *nothing* in that message that could be good. Carter has to be completely and totally enraged right now, thinking I made up the lies on purpose. Spread them as some kind of revenge.

But maybe I can reply. Explain. I'll apologize and tell him that I never *said* he did it. That people saw me and just jumped to conclusions. I'll tell him how I'm going to fix it.

So I click on the message.

> You fucking bitch. I let you in my house and this is how you repay me? By LYING? You're going to tell everyone the truth. Or your life will be miserable—I promise you that. Today was just a taste of what's to come if you don't undo this.

I sit back and blink rapidly, rereading the message over and over.

What will he do if I see him in person? How can I go to school again without making it abundantly clear I never meant for this to happen? I pull my legs up into the chair with me and rest my chin on my knees, staring blankly at the screen, wishing I would have just told everyone the truth as soon as I heard those two girls in the bathroom.

I go back to my main page. Click on the little status-update box. With shaky fingers, I start typing.

> LISTEN UP: Carter didn't do anything wrong. I never said he raped me. Someone misunderstood things and spread a lie. CARTER DIDN'T DO IT.

I should have thought of this sooner. Tell the truth without facing anyone. Then I'll stay home tomorrow, make sure the truth has enough time to make the rounds. By the time I go to school again, it'll be old news. This whole thing will just...go away. I grab the mouse and move it to the "submit" button.

I stop short of clicking it, the arrow simply hovering right over "submit." What will Nick do if he finds out this way?

But I have to do it, and all I keep doing is putting it off. I'll post this here right now, and that will *force* me to walk back over to his house and spill the truth before he sees it here and it's worse. This is my guarantee—once I've posted it here, I can't back out of telling the truth.

My finger trembles as I move it to the button.

A bubble pops up in the corner of the screen. An instant message.

Listen, skank.

I jerk back so fast my chair rolls away from the desk, and I have to scoot forward again and lean in to see the message. It's Carter. His golden hair beams at me from his tiny little user-icon, that same perfect smile spanning from ear to ear, showing off his flawless teeth.

My life is hell right now because of what you've done.
Fix it now or I'll fix it for you, and it won't be pretty.

Whoa.

YOU threw yourself at ME, and I didn't want you, or
    don't you remember that part?

I swallow. I never threw myself at him. But I do remember his ugly sneer as he laughed at me, running his fingers through that perfect hair of his. I remember the cruel tone to his voice as he called me a two-bagger. I remember the gleam in his eyes, his arrogance unhidden.

I slide my chair back, away from the computer, listening as the IM box beeps over and over as he floods my page with a flurry of angry comments. *Ping. Ping. Ping. Ping. Ping.*

The comments scroll by so fast I can't read them, not that I'm trying.

I picture that girl in the parking lot, her emerald eyes glimmering with tears as she recounted the way Carter mocked her, his group of goonies cackling right along with him. I think of Tracey, who gave him her virginity only to be dumped. I think of the way his eyes lingered on my upper thighs, that smirk on his lips, before he told me I was too ugly to get with. I think of the word "whore" emblazoned on my locker, for everyone to see.

And then, as an overwhelming wave of fury overtakes me, I pull my chair closer to the desk and start typing.

I didn't do this to you. But you know what? You kinda
    deserve it.

I hit "send," and then sign out before he can respond.

Thirteen

The next morning, I take almost an hour to get ready. I can barely brush my teeth without gagging because I'm so nauseated, and I can't get my hair in a straight ponytail because my hands are shaking so badly. What was I thinking, yesterday? Carter has more power in his pinky than I have in my whole body. A whole clique of friends—entire sports teams—have his back.

I sit down on my bed for a second and stare at my computer. It's not too late to log on and post the message. I should do it, right now, before things get worse.

But instead of opening my laptop, I just sit and stare at the computer from across the room, my feet tapping on the floor. Carter went off on me and cussed me out for something I didn't even do. And he's messed with a lot of people. Used them to get what he wants, or laughed right in their faces. He walks around like everyone owes him something, like he's some kind of god and we're just the peasants, there for his use. Disposable.

Maybe he can squirm, just for one more day, and then I'll fix it. I give the laptop one last lingering look and then get to my feet.

———————

I'm only halfway down the front steps before I stop. Nick is walking up my sidewalk.

"I thought you would want a ride," he says, shoving his hands into his pockets. He glances behind me, at the front door, as if concerned my dad might burst out.

I glance back, too. Dad *is* still inside. "Oh. Uh, you don't have any … activities after school?"

His face falls. "Oh. Um, yeah. A couple things for the graduation ceremonies."

"I can follow you."

"Yeah. That sounds good." He steps forward and, after glancing at my house to be sure Dad's not watching, gives me a quick hug.

We part and head to our cars, and I breathe a deep sigh once I'm in mine. I'll tell him when we get to school. I'll climb into his car and we'll talk, and then when I step into the halls, he'll either be with me or he won't.

We accelerate down the streets, weeks-old cherry blossoms swirling in the air around us. It would be pretty if my mood weren't so dark.

It doesn't take long for us to arrive, and I pull into an empty parking stall a few spaces down from him and jump out of my car. He's opening his door just as I get to the Mustang, but I slide in and shut the passenger door behind me. So he just settles back down and turns to me.

"You all right?" he asks, squeezing my shoulder.

"Um, okay, I guess." Not really. The panic rises in waves. I'm doing it. I'm going to tell him.

"You're not just saying that?"

I shake my head and swallow, trying to clear the boulder in my throat so that I don't stumble on my words.

"Do you want to go to the senior party together?"

I blink. "The senior party? Like a date?"

He smiles. "Yeah. Basically."

My jaw drops. "Yeah. I mean, I'd love to."

"Great."

I feel like my stomach's dropped out completely.

"I can't believe we graduate this weekend," he adds. "It always seemed so far away, and now, here it is."

I twist around in my seat and lean against the headrest. We sort of lean into each other, drawn together like magnets. "I know, it's like—"

At *tap tap tap*, I jerk upright, my heart pounding wildly. Then I remember ... we're not at home, we're at school, so it can't possibly be my dad.

Nick visibly swallows and then clicks the button for

the window, and I wait, my heart in my throat, as it lowers, the tint giving away to the early spring sunshine.

All I see is the letterman jacket, and my grip on the door tightens, especially when I see the baseball symbol inside the letter, four slashes next to it. A senior. A guy who has lettered in baseball every year.

Carter.

But when he ducks down, I see it's only Gary, a guy who has been on the team with Carter every year. My stomach unclenches as he squats alongside the Mustang with his forearms resting on the windowsill. My relief that it's not Carter doesn't last long. Because he's still one of Carter's crew.

I feel myself break into a sweat, my skin too warm, the collar of my T-shirt too tight. He opens his mouth to talk to Nick, and then his eyes sweep toward me and he stops.

And then I know. He didn't expect me to be here, because he freezes for a long second before recovering. "Hey Sam, you doing okay?"

His voice is soft, quiet, like he's afraid I'm going to bolt at any second. I guess it's my death grip on the door handle. I nod but I don't speak because I can barely swallow. Gary is in my AP chemistry class. We've been lab partners several times.

He looks me dead in the eyes. "Um, I was just going to talk to Nick. About, you know, making sure he watches out for you. I wanted to make sure you didn't think we were…" His voice trails off a bit and he swallows, shifts around. "All on Carter's side. Just because we're on the same team."

I can't move.

Gary turns to Nick. "I know how Carter is with girls. What he'll do to get what he wants. I have to listen to it every day. Do you know he told Tracey Pearson he loved her just so she'd finally give it up? Some of the guys applauded him, even after they found out he dumped her. And yet still, I never thought he'd go this far..." His voice turns whispery and he glances at me. Like I haven't overheard the whole thing.

My breathing gets shallow. This is surreal. I hardly know this guy and he believes me even when he shouldn't. Why do people trust me like this? Why do they believe the things I'm saying? They shouldn't. They should trust Carter, the only guy in this school who really matters to anyone.

Nick darts a glance over at me.

"You don't have to talk about me like I'm not sitting right here," I say.

Gary looks back at Nick. "Look, I wasn't going to say anything, but I heard the guys talking last night and they're going to retaliate. And I thought you needed to know." He clears his throat. "I was just going to tell you so that you could, you know, protect her or something."

It's like all the blood drains from my body at once. Gary stands. "Just keep an eye on her, okay?"

I can't see his face now that he's standing, just his letterman jacket. And then he whirls and stalks off, just as a deep rumbling sounds through the air. I twist in my seat and see the big black Charger pulling into the lot. He must have washed it, because I don't see any streaks of yellow.

I struggle with my seat belt. Carter. Oh God, it's Carter. My hands can't find the buckle.

"*Sam*," Nick says.

I jerk and twist and pound at it, my heart climbing right into my throat and strangling me.

"*Sam*," Nick repeats. A frantic plea twists free of my throat as I jerk hard on the buckle.

"*Sam!*"

I still at the bite in his voice.

"Calm down. You're in my car. Carter won't expect you to be in here. And the windows are tinted." There's an edge to his voice I didn't expect. An odd, growling sort of tone. He hits the button and the window goes up.

A chill sweeps over me. He thinks I'm freaking out because Carter raped me and that's why I'm terrified of him.

I twist around in my seat, stare at Nick. "Sorry."

He leans back in. "You don't owe me an apology."

"But I do," I say. Words swirl around me, but the ones I need fail to materialize. How can I say it in a way that will make him understand? "All of this has gotten so ... out of hand."

I twist around, watch through his back window as Carter climbs out of his car, just a half-dozen parking spaces from us. He slams the door as his buddy climbs out of the passenger seat, and the two cross the gravel lot.

He still has that swagger of his, the way he ambles toward school as if he owns it.

I can't take my eyes off him. He glances to his left, and then to his right, shoving his hands into the pockets of his letterman jacket. We watch in silence as he crosses the lawn toward the back entry of the school.

"He looks nervous," Nick says, as I slide deeper into my seat.

"Yeah, I was just thinking that."

"I'll go talk to him," he says, pulling the keys from the ignition.

"Don't!" I say, too loud. I drop my voice. "Please. Just… it's not necessary."

"Sam, how can you just let him get away with this? Someone needs to—"

"Listen to me, Nick." My stomach rises toward my throat. I have to tell him now, before we walk into school. "The thing is…" I rake in a deep breath of air. "Carter—"

The shrill sound of the bell interrupts me.

"Crap, I still need to get a book out of my locker," Nick says. "Can we walk and talk?"

"Oh, uh, sure."

I climb out of the car, pulling my backpack over my shoulders as we go.

"What were you saying?"

The courage I had in the car falters. Students scurry past us, worried about being late. I have three, four minutes tops, before the next bell rings. Nick hates being late.

He's received an attendance award every quarter for as long as I've known him.

"Nothing," I say, as we reach the doors. "Can we catch up later?"

———————

My Chem final is a disaster. Gary is sitting next to me and he keeps darting concerned, sad little looks at me. Like he'll actually be able to see the cracks in my façade spreading if he watches closely enough. All it does is strengthen my resolve to pretend like nothing is wrong.

I fill in the last five multiple-choice answers without reading the questions. The words aren't really registering anyway, so what's the point?

The speaker in the back corner of the room crackles to life. I twist in my seat and look at the big black box. "Samantha Marshall, please report to the principal's office."

I tense. Crap. Crap. Crap. They must have figured out about my skipping class on Monday, when I ran from the bathroom stall and never went back to school. I never should have done that. Another broken rule. What's with me? Can I get in serious trouble this close to the end of the year?

Everyone swivels in their seats to stare at me, two dozen sets of intensely curious expressions. I'm not the sort of girl to get in trouble. Until now. I reach over and grab my backpack, my chair creaking. I loop my arms through the straps and nod at the teacher as I head to the door. I'm walking like entering the hall is stepping onto a gangplank. Who knows what's at the other end?

What am I going to tell the principal? I need an excuse for ditching, but I don't think there is one. It's not like the school can expel me three days before graduation. Right?

Even so, I've never been in trouble, and my stomach continues to knot as I wander down the hall. This is probably going to mar my record. But I guess it doesn't matter. I'm only going to UW, unlike Yale-bound Nick. My heart twists as I think of it. Who is going to show up at noon when he realizes I stayed home sick, and rifle through my cupboards until he finds a can of chicken noodle soup?

The big wooden door is propped open, and I pass the little secretary desk and stand in the entry to Mr. Paulson's office. He's seated behind an enormous oak desk, a shiny brass nameplate in front proudly proclaiming his title. A wilted fern decorates the opposite corner. A battered wooden shelf unit fills up one wall, books and binders crammed into it. The blinds are pulled up and the early summer sun streams through, illuminating the dust suspended in midair.

"Take a seat, Miss Marshall."

I chew on my bottom lip as I plunk down in the chair opposite his desk, trying desperately to appear casual and unconcerned. I need some kind of plan, some pressing reason for fleeing campus. A flu bug? Should have gone to the nurse. An emergency at home? He'll want to verify that with my dad.

"Do you know why I've called you here?"

I shake my head. Play innocent.

"It's come to my attention—"

His phone rings. I nearly jump out of my seat. He holds up a finger in the "one minute" symbol. "Paulson."

He's nodding his head, listening to the faint buzz in the receiver. "Uh-huh. Sure. Three o'clock. See you then."

The receiver slams down and he turns his attention back to me. I cross my legs and then uncross them. Sit up straighter.

"As I was saying. It's come to my attention that your locker was vandalized."

I think I might sink right into the floor. This isn't about my truancy?

"It was fixed, of course, by our custodial staff." He pauses and I guess my nod tells him that I've seen it. "Do you have any idea why someone would have done such a thing?"

I swallow and shake my head, wringing my hands. "Um, no, I don't know who did it," I say.

He stares at me for a long moment, leaning on his elbow, his eyes narrowed. It's impossible not to gulp. Does he know I'm lying?

"Vandalism does not occur at MHS," he says. "And this is … particularly vulgar."

I widen my eyes and nod, pray I look more innocent than panicked.

"Let's hope this is the last, and only incident. You may return to class."

It's hard not to leap out of the chair and scurry out before he has a chance to look into my attendance. I'm out in the hallways before I can even take a breath.

I tighten the straps on my backpack as I turn right, toward the cafeteria. The shrill bell rings out all around me and the doors fling open, students streaming into the halls, filling the place with an audible hum. I pick up my pace. I don't want to run into half of the students at this school. Not the football players, the basketball players, the baseball players. I'm not sure I ever realized the influence Carter had over this school.

I do now.

An arm loops around mine and before I can react, I'm yanked out a side door. I am about to spin and launch myself on the stranger, but then I see Veronica's face.

"Carter was up ahead," she hisses, dragging me into the courtyard. "You seriously need to pay more attention."

"Oh."

"You okay?"

I groan. "Must everyone ask me that over and over?"

She cringes. "Sorry, we're all just worried about you."

"Who is *we*?"

"Macy and Tracey and me. We were talking about it, and we think the four of us should meet up after school. Grab something to eat in town or something."

I raise a brow. "Are you sure? I'm not convinced they actually like me ... "

She nods. "Yeah. I mean, they really care about what's going on with you."

I chew on my lip, trying to hide the guilt. Nothing is going on with me. But Veronica looks strangely hopeful. Excited, maybe. "Really? You want to go?" I ask.

"Yeah. And I think it would do you some good."

"Okay. Sure. I just have to text my dad."

"Awesome. I'll drive. Meet me in the senior lot at three."

————

"Let me just ditch my backpack in my car and we can go," I say as Veronica and I walk across the gravel parking lot.

"Sure," she says, nodding.

A few beats of silence stretch between us before she stops walking. "You drive a yellow car, don't you?" she asks.

I look up to see a group of guys walking away from my car. Baseball guys, long and muscular, easy to spot in their letterman jackets and ball caps. They saunter by, looking as if they own the world. Brent, the guy from the courtyard, holds up his key ring and jingles it, the gleam of arrogance in his eyes as he stares at me.

My eyes widen and I swallow, look over at my car.

Slut.

"Holy shit," Veronica says. "I can't believe they'd do that!" She whirls around as if to go after them, but doesn't actually move. Instead, she reaches out and gives my arm a squeeze.

It's carved right into the driver's side door, with an arrow pointing up. So that when I'm sitting in the driver's seat, it will point right at me. My hand flutters to my mouth and the nausea that just won't quit swells again. I blink hard to keep the tears where they belong. What did I do to deserve this? *Any* of this?

One of the guys lets out a catcall and I twist around, see him making some kind of obscene gesture with his hand near his crotch, and then they disappear, proud of what they've done.

They're taking Carter's side. They don't even know if it's true or not, they're just taking his side. Maybe they don't even care if it's true—they just want to screw with me.

I'm hit with the horrifying realization of what this would do to me if it really was true ... If I really was ...

A victim.

They would do this no matter what. They'd take Golden Boy's side and they'd ruin me. If it had really happened, I would shatter into a thousand pieces.

But you're not a victim.

"Are you ... "

I dig my own keys out of my pocket as the tears shimmer, burst free. Frantically, I scurry to my car and scrape at the metal. My hands shake as hard as my heart beats, my fingers gripping the keys so tightly they ache. Back and forth, back and forth, until I've gouged so much paint off the door that the word is no longer legible. Yellow paint flecks litter the ground around us.

Veronica clears her throat but doesn't speak. We just stand there for a second, staring at the bare metal on the car door. "So ... that sucks."

I nod, feeling defeated. "Yeah. Let's just go. I'll deal with it later." I toss my backpack into my car and then click the lock button, following her over to her own car which, thankfully, is vandalism free. It's all I can do to keep my breathing under control.

"Are you sure you're okay? Maybe we should stay and file a report or something."

With who? My dad?

"No, really, let's just get out of here." I pull my phone out to fire off a text to my dad, then turn my phone off.

"Okay, suit yourself," she says, unlocking her own car.

I pull the door open and sink into the bucket seat of her little Chevy, buckling in as she tosses her backpack into the messy back seat. "You okay with pizza? Tracey wanted something cheesy so she was going to meet us at the place in town. Hope that's cool."

I nod. "Sure."

The car fills with silence as she pulls out of the lot, heading toward the pizza and pasta joint where half the school hangs out. Neither of us speak as we cross town, and by the time we get to the restaurant, the silence is heavier than ever.

Tracey and Macy are already here, climbing out of Tracey's jeep. She gives me a bright smile and a wave as she heads toward us.

"Hey guys!"

"Hi," I say, chewing on my lip. This is weird. Uncomfortable. Nick's been my only friend for so long, and no one has ever really cared to invite me to things. And now

I'm having dinner with three girls who've hardly looked my way for the last few years.

I fidget under their gaze, glad they're more intent on pizza than me, because a moment later we're seated in a booth, menus spread out in front of us. I keep staring at it, even though I know all I want is Hawaiian.

"Did you see Matt Lewis's hat today?" Macy asks.

I look up and shake my head.

"It was this hideous orange newsboy thing. Seriously, you should have seen it. Truly heinous."

I laugh, which surprises even me.

"I like your shoes," Tracey says, nodding at the ballet flats I'm wearing. They're plain brown with a silver buckle on the toe.

"Oh, uh, thanks." I smile, a little uncomfortably, and busy myself with unwrapping the straw and putting it into my water glass. I never know what to do when someone actually compliments me. Thank them? Compliment them back?

"So what are we going to do about Carter?" Macy asks.

I narrow my eyes. "What do you mean?"

"Well, we heard about him freaking out on you in the hall. And so Tracey and I talked about it over lunch, and something needs to be done. You should feel safe in the halls at school, not like he might attack you again at any moment."

"Brent just keyed her car, too," Veronica adds.

"That's messed up," Tracey says. "We really should do something."

"Oh, uh…" I let out a bark of uncomfortable laughter. "I mean, I don't know that there's anything we can really do, you know? And it's not like he'd really attack me at school.

"But it's not just about what he did to you," Tracey says.

"It's not?"

She shakes her head. "No. It's about what he does to *everyone*. I spent the entire weekend in the bathroom after he dumped me, pretending to give myself a spa weekend so that my mom wouldn't come in and see my bloodshot eyes from crying. I had to keep the tub on for an hour to cover up the sounds of my sobbing as I lay on the floor, curled in a ball. And you know what Carter did?"

She purses her lips, raising one brow and staring me down. "He went camping with his guy friends, and they ended up *getting together* with some girls from the camp next door. I heard all about it on Monday at school."

Macy leans in. "And even though I wouldn't sleep with him, he told everyone I did."

I lean back. How can he be this guy *and* the one who has such a golden boy reputation? How could I have missed things that should have been so obvious?

I sigh. "I think we should just let this all blow over, you know?" I let out a weird hiccup of laughter and wave my hand around in the air.

"*Blow over*? After what he did to you? What he's done to all of us? The guy deserves a little bit of what he's got coming to him," Tracey says.

My mouth goes dry, tastes chalky. "Uh, what does he have coming to him?"

Tracey and Macy look at each other and smile. I dart my eyes over to Veronica, but she's just nodding her head.

"Wait, what do *you* have against Carter?"

She gives me a pointed look. "Don't tell me you didn't hear the rumors about me freshman year."

"That's when we were friends. And no."

"Spring of freshman year."

"Oh." My mouth goes dry. I did hear *some* rumors about her, but they were so beyond ridiculous I never gave them a second thought.

She stares for a long second. Then she rolls her eyes. "Carter asked me out." She pauses. "What? Don't look so shocked. Anyway, he wasn't a god yet. He's not my type either way, so I said no, and he told everyone I was a lesbian."

I choke on the water I'm sipping. Yeah, those were the rumors I heard, but I just dismissed them. Sort of. Maybe I almost believed them, because Veronica started getting into feminism. But I never thought they had anything to do with Carter. I never thought someone started them maliciously.

Maybe that's the point.

"I've spent the last three years getting harassed about that. And no one *ever* asks me out, because they think it's true. I'm going to graduate high school and I've never been kissed."

"Oh." God, is that really true? The more I know the

Carter that other people know, the more I hate myself for falling for his façade. But he was the villain the whole time. The idea makes my stomach churn.

"So anyway," Tracey says, "we were all talking, and we think you need to press charges. You might be able to get an emergency restraining order or something, so you wouldn't have to worry about him. And then he couldn't go to graduation or the party. You'd be safe that way."

My stomach drops like a lead weight. "I can't do that. I can't take *graduation* from him."

Macy leans in. "It might be harder to get because you didn't go to the police right away, but we think it's important. You need to report him. It's not okay for him to get away with this."

It's hard not to dart my eyes away. Instead, I meet hers. "No. I don't want this to be bigger than it already is, and if I did that, it'll just be more difficult for me. Everyone already knows, and they stare at me. In the halls, in the cafeteria, in class."

"This is important," Veronica says. "Wouldn't you feel guilty if it happened to someone else, and you could have stopped it? You need to be brave for a while longer and go to the police."

Macy gets this soft look on her face and reaches out, resting her hands on mine. There's something off about all this. "Sweetie, it happened. Not pressing charges doesn't mean it will go away. We'll go with you, if you want."

I pull my hand away, feeling sick to my stomach, the world pressing down on me. All of them are here right now because they think Carter wronged me like he wronged them. They don't know I'm already ruining him. They think Carter is capable of rape and they're here to somehow fix it for me. They want to help me get over something that never really happened.

I'm disgusted with myself. And I can't do this any longer.

"I can't press charges," I insist.

"You have to," Tracey says.

"But he didn't do it," I blurt. Instantly, my cheeks flame hot. I swallow, glancing nervously from one girl to the next, ready to leap to my feet and run.

The three of them exchange looks again. "What?" Veronica finally says.

"He never..." My voice comes out shaky, unstable. I lower my voice, rest my hands in my lap because they're trembling out of control. "Raped me."

Macy stares at me as she sips her water, and Tracey sits back in her chair. "But—"

"Have you girls decided what you want?"

I stare at my lap as the waitress scribbles down the pizza order, my cheeks still burning. The girls stare right at me, waiting. When she finally leaves, I want to go with her.

"So you just... made it up?" Tracey asks.

I shake my head. "It wasn't like that. Someone else started the rumor. When Veronica asked me if it was really true, I didn't even know what she meant. I was too embarrassed to ask, so I just nodded my head."

Tracey leans in. "But why? If you never accused him of that, why did everyone think that?"

I chew on my lip. "I was drinking, and I *never* drink. I went into his room and I tripped, and my shirt ripped on the handle to his dresser and I bruised my cheek. He helped me up..." I dart a look at Tracey. "He thought I went into his room to throw myself at him, or something. And I didn't, not really. But he told me I was too ugly to hook up with. I followed him out of his room in tears and Michelle Pattison saw me and must have started the rumor."

The silence lingers forever, but it feels good to finally let it out. How can I tell the truth to three girls I hardly know, and not to my best friend?

Tracey crosses her arms as her gaze lingers on my face. "And you went along with it?"

I swallow, nodding. "When you two came up to me in the cafeteria, I still had no clue what you guys thought Carter did. I was just nodding to get rid of you. It was at least an hour later before I overheard some girls in the bathroom and realized what everyone was saying."

I feel shaky, weak, unsure, ready to run all the way home if all this goes wrong. I never planned to tell them this, and what will they do? Rush back to school and tell everyone I'm a big fat liar? Retaliate, on Carter's behalf? Hate me?

"I swear to you, if I'd understood what people thought had happened, I would have set them straight immediately," I finish. "But by the time I figured it out, it seemed too hard to fix it."

They all sit back, exchange glances. Veronica picks up a fork and kind of spins it around. Tracey chews on her lips as she stares down at her nails. The silence is heavy enough to choke on, and I just want to slide under the table, hide out until this is all over.

"Wow," Tracey finally says.

"Yeah. Wow," Macy chimes in.

Veronica just keeps spinning the fork.

Macy lets out a long, slow sigh. "You know what's weird, though?"

I shrug, feeling kind of nauseated now.

"I never doubted it." She glances over at Tracey. "As soon as I heard the rumors, I totally believed them."

"Me too."

"Me three," Veronica says, looking kind of sheepish.

"That's pretty bad," Macy says, turning back to me. "That we didn't even consider whether he might be innocent."

Tracey gives her a look. "It's not our fault, it's his. I mean, if he's the kind of person who makes it easy for everyone to believe it, he's not a very good guy."

Macy chews on her lip. "But shouldn't we have given him the benefit of the doubt? We're like a lynch mob or something, just believing it right away."

Tracey shakes her head. "No. I'm telling you, it's his *actions* that made the rumor believable. The things he's done to us. It's a given that we'd believe it, because we know who he is."

Veronica's lashes flare, and she seems to brighten. "Exactly. So you totally shouldn't feel *that* bad."

I shake my head. "I don't know that everyone believed it. They just like gossip."

Macy gives me *the look*. "They believed it. Trust me."

"I have to fix it, though. I just don't know how. The gossip spread so quickly and it's like it spiraled out of control, and I've been so afraid of telling anyone the truth."

"You don't have to tell anyone," Tracey says. Her eyes dart to Macy and Veronica. "It's about time Carter got what he deserves."

My jaw drops. "I can't do that. This is …" I lean in closer and lower my voice to a whisper. "This is *rape* we're talking about, not some petty rumor. It's serious."

She shrugs. "So? The guy's an asshole and he's spent his entire high school existence as some untouchable god, and he needs to be taken down a notch."

I clench my jaw. I can't believe this.

Or maybe I can. Didn't I think the same thing at some point? That he'd sort of earned this by everything he'd done? Hadn't I *said* that to him on Facebook?

But a couple days of lying and forever are two different things.

Aren't they?

"This isn't just a notch," I mumble. "It's rock bottom. Doesn't get much worse than this."

Tracey and Macy lean back and stare at me from across

the booth. A second ago they felt like allies, and now they look like it's me against them. "Did you know he's moving to California right after graduation?" Tracey asks. "No one will care about some stupid high school rumors. Two more days, Sam. Then graduation, and he's home free. Carter can handle a few freakin' days where he's not worshipped by everyone in a hundred-mile radius. Then he moves away and this all disappears."

And this all disappears.

"But, it's not right," I say, my voice no longer quite so resolute.

"And it's right to let him walk around as if he's Mother freakin' Theresa? Come on, Sam. Take the easy route and let the rumor run its course. He'll move away, and you can go on with your life as if none of this ever happened."

As if none of this ever happened.

I swallow and look over at Veronica, who gives me a nod and a slight smile. "Please? I've spent three years dodging the rumors he created about me. This is just one week."

I clear my throat. "But people are vandalizing my locker. Threatening me."

"We'll have your back, and once school is over, they won't be around to do anything. And when Carter moves, they'll just forget about it."

"But if I agree, that means no more revenge. No retaliation beyond this rumor."

Maybe most of the people at school don't believe it anyway. It's just a rumor. Maybe it's harmless. I can handle the threats and harassment for a couple more days, if it means avoiding the truth. Then the rumor will die down and everyone will forget about it.

Tracey and Macy exchange another one of their glances, and then beam at me. "Deal."

Relief swoops through me. I don't have to face it head on. It just goes away when Carter leaves town.

Just like I wanted.

Fourteen

This morning I found another note in my locker, one that simply says *Tell the fucking truth*, but otherwise, I've managed to avoid Carter today. He can't figure out what to do to me during class, so all I get is harsh glares. In the halls we've had at least three near-misses, but he hasn't been able to confront me. It's working. Carter's at arm's length, and graduation is the day after tomorrow.

I'm tired, though. My feet shuffle across the halls. My notebooks are empty and I haven't slept, either. I spent last night staring at the ceiling.

When I'm called into the principal's office for the second time this week, I can't even pretend to be surprised.

My fingers now know the cold steel of the doorknob, my body knows the discomfort of the stiff leather chairs. And thus I find myself sitting down, crossing my ankles, faking as if I'm prim and proper and perfect when I'm anything but.

I clasp my hands in my lap and wait for Mr. Paulson to call me on all the things I've done this week. Wait for him to suspend me, to expel me, to tell me he knows what a monumental fraud I am. I've skipped class, caused alterations in the halls…

"I'm sorry to see you in here again so soon," he says, leaning back in his high-backed chair.

I swallow, hard, and study his cool expression. Where before he'd been so friendly and accommodating, today he seems suspicious, his head tipped to the side. I slide down in my chair, lean back against the cracked leather and pretend to be unworried, but it's nearly impossible, because it means my hands can't tremble and I can't chew on my lip or pull my fleece sweater tighter around me. It means I have to sit there, stiff and yet faking that it's natural.

He straightens his tie, an ugly blue plaid thing that belongs in the trash bin. "A student has just informed me that your car was vandalized. And your locker has been vandalized yet again."

I'm surprised he knows the car damage happened on school grounds. Someone must have seen the guys before I showed up. Crap. I breathe deeply and nod.

Today, my locker says *skank*. Not marker, this time,

but actual scratches in the brand-new gray paint. Deep, ugly gouges.

Gouges I deserve.

"I've looked up your attendance, Miss Marshall. I was not pleased to discover you've missed a couple of your courses this week. With unexcused absences."

It's all I can do not to shift in my chair, bite my lip. Instead I stare straight ahead, almost unblinking, and simply nod again, a stiff, unnatural move.

He clears his throat, then leans forward and stares me down, intense, demanding. A look that would work in an FBI interrogation room. "Now, would you like to tell me if these issues are, perhaps, related? Your normal attendance record is nearly flawless, and you've never had any behavioral issues."

I can't meet his eyes. I stare out the window, at the little apple tree blowing gently in the breeze, the pink blossoms drifting silently away from the windows. I want to be outside leaning against that tree, my eyes shut, the world far enough away that I don't have to think about it.

Mr. Paulson's chair creaks as he leans back, crosses his arms at his chest. "Miss Marshall, this is a small school. It's quite easy to know when something is afoot."

I turn away from the window and look at him. "I'm not sure I know what you mean."

"You were in a verbal altercation recently with Carter Wellesley."

My heart slams into my throat.

"If your personal relationships cause issues under this

roof, I will cause issues for your pristine school record. Do we have an understanding?"

I nod.

"One more incident, with either of you, and I'll dig much deeper than you want me to. I'll see to it that one of you—both of you—see consequences. I don't care who. Just as long as these problems go away. Vandalism, disrespect—it's not okay in this school."

I nod, perhaps too enthusiastically, wanting desperately for this whole thing to just ... be over.

"Mossyrock is an idyllic community, Miss Marshall, and I won't have you disrupt that."

I nod again, vigorously, desperate for him to shut up.

"Very well. You may go. But one more problem ... even the tiniest of problems, and I expect to see you sitting in that chair again."

"No problems. I promise," I say, darting for the door. "Thanks, Mr. Paulson."

I let go of the breath I'm holding as I bound down the halls, feeling like an escaped jailbird. That was close. Really, really close.

I just have to get through one more day of school. But the principal knows enough to realize something is off. Does everyone else know, too? Do they realize I've lied to them all this time?

I shake my head. That's stupid. They believe me, not Carter. They believe the rumor, not Carter. Two more days and I'm scot-free. Two more days and we graduate, and Carter goes off to California, and it's all over.

Two more days, and the lie won't matter anymore.

———————

Back home after school, dressed in sweats, I'm eating cereal hunched over on a chair so I can rest my chin on my knees, when Dad walks in through the door wearing his full police garb. My breath catches. I'd hoped he wouldn't be home until I was in bed. I don't want to talk to him.

"Hey Dad," I say, slurping milk from my spoon, eyeballing him as discreetly as possible. He doesn't look irate, so he still must not have seen the vandalism on my car door.

"Cereal for dinner?"

I shrug. "It sounded good."

He holds up the mail. "You got something."

A tingle goes down my spine as I recognize the purple emblem on the corner of the envelope. The thick envelope. Good God, why didn't I think to check the mail?

"Care to tell me anything?"

My mouth goes dry, and I shrug as if there's nothing weird about getting a thick, eight-by-eleven envelope from a college he doesn't think I'm attending. "No."

I try to take another spoonful of Froot Loops–flavored milk, but my hand shakes and the milk spills off.

I evade his looks and try again, until I hear *rippp* and I realize he's opening up the envelope. I shove my chair back but I'm not there before he's reading the letter.

"Enclosed please find our student survey," he reads. "This is necessary to assign you an appropriate roommate

155

in the dormitory. We are asking that you return the survey by June 31st."

When he lowers the letter and looks at me, his eyes are blazing.

"Dorm room assignments?"

I swallow and just stare.

"Go get the rest of it."

"The rest of what?"

"The paperwork. If they're assigning a dorm, that means you're registered. So get me the paperwork. *Now*," he spits out, his chest beginning to heave with anger.

Fear surges through me, but I refuse to give it away. I cross my arms at my chest and raise my chin a notch. "We never agreed on anything," I say. "I chose UW."

"I'm not paying for you to attend UW. It's in Seattle. It's not safe, it's too far, and too expensive."

"I don't need your money. I have financial aid."

He snorts, strides away from me, and stares out the window for a long, dark moment. "You can't have received financial aid. I would have had to give you my information—social security number, income, everything."

I purse my lips. "You did. Last year, when I filled out the FAFSA, remember?"

He whirls around, his face turning red. Oh God, he's getting angry. *Seriously* angry. My stomach flops over.

"That was for community college," he grinds out.

I shrug, hope he doesn't see the cracks in my façade. "I added UW."

He slams the envelope down on the table. "You lied to me!"

Desperation chokes me. "I tried to tell you, but you never want to talk to me!"

"Because you're not going!" he roars.

"Yes I am!" I say, my voice raspy, pathetic. He can't do this. He can't take it away from me. If Nick leaves and all I do is stay here, I'm clinching my fate as a nobody, a dead-ender, forever.

"You can't put yourself through college just on financial aid. You're going to need cash. Living expenses."

I nod. "I have enough saved to get me through the first quarter, and I'll get a job … "

He steps forward, staring down at me, and I shrink back a step. "You are not going to UW. End of story. You *will* attend CCC, as discussed." He rips up the student survey as I feel my eyes moisten, watch everything I've ever wanted shred before my eyes. "If you push me on this, you *will* regret it."

He stomps on the pedal to the garbage can, and when the lid snaps up, he drops the shreds into it and it clangs shut.

"Give me the rest of it," he says, his voice hard.

"Dad—"

"Now!"

Tears trickle down my cheeks. "Why do you have to be like this?"

"Like what? I'm being practical, and I'm protecting

you, but you're too young to see it. Now go get me the paperwork."

"I hate you," I whisper, then twist around and race up the steps, slamming my door behind me and locking it. I find my paperwork and rush to the closet, shoving it under some clothes in the back where he won't find it.

Then I throw myself on the bed and cry.

———————

A half hour later, I watch my dad back his blue police cruiser out of our driveway. He must have been on break or something. He would take his personal car if he wasn't going back to work.

I wait five minutes, then I slip out the front door, crossing the lawn in mere seconds.

The grass at Nick's house hasn't been maintained by the perfect lawn sculpting crew, like ours, and thus has a few weeds sprouting. I hop up onto his cedar front porch and don't bother ringing the bell. At Nick's house, you just walk in.

I push the door open and turn left, toward the stairs, which I take two-by-two. Downstairs, I can hear his mom and dad talking while his mom cooks, probably something homey like a pasta salad or ham sandwiches or something.

For the thousandth time, I wish I lived here. It's a dull ache that grows in my chest, a little more every day. I'll never know what it's like to grow up somewhere like this. That chance is over. Crushed. My dad doesn't know, doesn't care. Doesn't anything. Someday I'll finally move away, and then what? Then I have no one.

I tap twice on Nick's door before shoving it open. Nick is on his computer, leaning back in his black desk chair. It's not much different than the image he must have seen when he walked into *my* room last weekend. Before everything went to hell.

It's nice being so close. Repeating history. Understanding each other. But now there's a secret between us and I still hope it doesn't tear the whole thing apart.

"Hey," I say, falling onto his bed. He turns around. I contemplate tossing a pillow at him to incite another wrestling match. If I thought it would go that route, I might do it. But everything is so complicated now.

"What's up?" He twists around, pulling his feet up onto his chair and giving me *a look*. A look that says he wants to know how I'm doing, how I'm processing it all.

Because he thinks I was raped last weekend.

"Not much." I shrug, lean back against the mound of pillows on his bed. "I'm just glad to be done with finals." I sink back, wish I could just pull a blanket over my head and cuddle in deeper.

"Yeah? Me too."

I let out a long, slow sigh. "Are you ready to move on from all this?"

"Uh, yeah. I'm dying for Yale."

I frown. "Why? Is this town so bad? Are you so eager to leave … " My voice trails off and I wave my hands around. "This?"

Why am I even asking him this? *I'm* eager to leave it too. But Nick's going to Yale and I'm going…to UW. I think. God, after today, I don't even know any more. I told myself I'd go no matter what he said, swore it didn't matter how he reacted, I still would go. But now I don't know if I can do it. Be all on my own like that, my dad royally pissed. Nick across the country. A stranger for a roommate. The closer it gets, the more implausible it seems.

Some part of me is desperate for Nick to tell me to skip UW. For him to beg me to follow him.

I'd do it, if only he'd ask.

"Leave you? Not so much. Everything else? Sure."

"But why? You have it good. You have *everything*," I say, my voice a touch too envious. "What's so bad about all this?"

He shrugs, and for a second it's like this whole convo bores him. "I just want more. I want to see the rest of the country. I want to be challenged. I want…*more*," he repeats.

It deflates me. Even without all the lies that will soon push us apart, I know I could never be enough for him.

"You can't tell me an old logging town is really enough for you," he says. "Aren't you pumped to go to UW?"

"My dad says I'm not going," I say.

"Why?"

I sit up. "He wants me to go to community college and live at home, so he can keep an eye on me."

"Why is he like that? You've never gotten in any kind

of trouble. Does he think he can bubble-wrap the world in the next two years while keeping you at home?"

I shrug. "I don't know. Maybe."

"You *are* going to follow through with it, right? Just like you always said?"

I worry my bottom lip. "I … "

"Sam! Promise me you're not going to cave in again."

"What do you mean, *again*?"

Nick gives me an exasperated look. "In sixth grade, he didn't want you to go to camp, so you stayed home. In eighth, you skipped the class trip to Olympia because he didn't think it had sufficient chaperones. You didn't get your license until you were seventeen, even though you had saved enough to buy a car. You didn't participate in Senior Skip Day because you were afraid he'd catch you. You're *going* to UW. You're not giving this up for him."

"Easy for you to say," I grumble.

"What?"

I throw my hands up in the air. "You go over there and tell him that! You go live in my room and I'll live in yours and you see how long you can be so cavalier about your decisions!"

Nick has the audacity to look exasperated. "Why do you let him have so much power?"

Argh! "Because he *has* it! That's why!"

"No one can make you feel—"

"*Inferior without your consent.* Yeah, I know, Mr. Wise-guy. But it's not as easy as you think," I say, my voice dripping with desperation. "Do you remember that summer I wore sneakers to the beach?"

He raises a brow.

"It's because we went sandal shopping and I insisted on these jelly sandals because they were cute and glittery, but he told me they'd break. He only relented because I begged and people were watching. They broke in two days but he refused to buy me any sandals because I was supposed to *live with my choice*. It seems so stupid and trivial, but it's how he does everything. He wants to control what I do, and when he can't, he punishes me. If I don't go where he wants me to go, he'll figure out how to make my life hell."

Nick shakes his head, and he has the gall to look like he feels sorry for me. "It's not all about him, Sam."

"How is it not about him?" I ask, my fingers digging into my palms.

"You always take the easiest path. You make your choices by default."

"What does that even mean?"

"You let people decide everything for you. I mean God, we became best friends because I live next door and I was available. You could have made other friends, but you didn't."

"Don't throw that at me," I say, anger and defeat swirling inside me. He's right, I know he's right, but I desperately want to keep the anger.

"Why not? And even right now, are you with me because you want to be, or because I was the first person around when things with Carter went wrong?"

My jaw drops. I snap it shut, grinding my teeth. Then I stand up and whirl on him.

"I went after Carter to make you jealous because I couldn't tell you how I felt, okay?" I yell. "Does *that* make you feel better? I went into his room because I thought it was the easiest way to get you to finally see me as something other than a best friend."

His face goes white, and he blinks. Once, twice, three times. When he reaches for me, I pull away.

"I'm sorry, I—"

"I'll see you at school," I say, spinning around and leaving his room.

"Sam! I'm sorry!"

I pause in the door, feeling tears shimmer. "No, you're not. You're right. I can't seem to do anything for myself, and I sure as hell can't seem to get anything right."

Then I twist around and stumble down the stairs, rushing across the lawn and back to my house. My cell phone is already vibrating in my pocket, but I ignore it.

Fifteen

The last day of class. The fifth day of my lie. Or the seventh, if you count the days I didn't even know about it and everyone else did.

I'm only halfway down our carpeted stairs, my hand sliding along the golden-oak railing, when my dad appears at the foot of the steps, staring up at me.

"Anything you'd like to tell me about?" he asks.

There are about a hundred things going on, none of which I'd like to tell you, I think.

"Um … no?"

"So you weren't planning to tell me you damaged your car?"

Oh. "I didn't think it was a big deal—"

"When will you ever become a responsible person?" he barks. "What did you do? Smash into a pole or a tree or something?

"What? I *am* responsible!" I am, right? I get decent grades even though I'm not naturally gifted. I do my chores and keep my nose clean. Mostly. I push past him and grab my sneakers, sitting down at the dining room table and jamming my feet into them, anger boiling.

"This just proves my point. You think you can go gallivant off to college and you can't even be responsible for your car when you're still at home."

"I'm not going to *gallivant*—"

"Exactly. You're going to—"

I stand, then swipe my notebooks off the table and let them slam to the ground. And then I all but scream. "Dad!"

My chest heaving, we just stand there, staring at each other. "I am *going* to leave. Whether you like it or not."

I whirl around and leave him standing there, my books and papers cluttering the floor around him.

Someday he'll understand. If he doesn't break me first.

But it's not today. On either account.

———

At school, I wait impatiently between Tracey and Macy as the line in the cafeteria inches forward. I wish Nick was around right now. I need to talk to him, need to apologize for totally freaking out last night. But as class president, he has something to do. Related to graduation or the senior party or something.

"Seriously, you'd think they'd come up with a better method for distributing yearbooks than this. It's pathetic," Tracey says.

I nod. The cafeteria is crowded, and I can't stop scanning faces for familiar ones that belong to the jocks. To Carter's friends. At least this is the last day I'll need to creep around like some criminal. Which I suppose is ironic, since everyone thinks Carter is the criminal.

Macy is chewing on a straw. "My parents paid for one of those ads in the back, where they put in a baby photo. But they refused to say which one it was, and I'm going to scream if it's that mud-pie one they have on the mantle."

I snort, and Macy cracks a smile.

"I bet they added things like *My little girl, all grown up*," Macy says in this fake sappy voice. "With, like, hearts and daisies all over the border."

"God, my mom already showed me what she did. It's my ballet photo from second grade, with some poem about pursuing your dreams or some crap." Tracey crosses her arms. "What'd yours do?"

I cough. "Uh, nothing. I haven't seen my mom in years."

Tracey and Macy freeze. "Oh, God—"

"I'm so sorry—"

I shrug away their simultaneous apologies. "Totally not a big deal. I mean, she left a long time ago."

I try to picture my dad submitting some baby photo of me for the back of the yearbook, but I can't see it.

I hardly even have any baby photos. The ones I do have were almost entirely taken by other people. If he put any kind of phrase or statement with my photo, it would be something like "buck up" or "you're too old to cry."

Jesus, when I started my period he gave me ten dollars and told me to *ride my bike* to the corner store.

The line inches forward and we're finally standing in front of the table. We give our names to the faculty volunteers, and they cross our names off the list before handing us the books. I clutch mine to my chest and follow Tracey and Macy to the opposite end of the cafeteria. On the last day of school every year, the seniors have all this free time for "School Spirit Activities," which really translates to absolutely nada other than yearbook-signing time and a lame end-of-year assembly.

I probably should have skipped.

I sit down at a round table with my back to the windows, across from the girls, and set my backpack on the floor. I open up the yearbook and quickly flip to the senior section, my lip curling when I see my picture staring back at me. Ugh. Dad had refused to shell out for the fancy photos most of the seniors get "when a perfectly good photographer comes to the school and takes your yearbook photo for free." God, I look horrible. My curls are all lopsided, hanging down further on one side than the other, and I have a big breakout on my chin. Yick.

I flip back a few pages and see Nick's perfect face

staring back at me. And sure enough, just like they all predicted, *Most likely to be President of the United States* is right under his photo.

I didn't get a superlative. Which is pathetic, when you figure there are at least twenty superlatives and only forty-five students. At least Allan Eldred, class nerd, got *Most likely to create the next Facebook.* And of course Carter received *Most likely to play a professional sport.*

Then again, after this week, maybe being invisible is better. At least I don't have these expectations.

I flip more pages and there's Carter, homecoming king. I glance up at Tracey. She's in the photo too, on his arm. I turn the page so she won't see what I'm looking at, but the next page isn't much better. There's a pull quote next to the football team's photo, where Carter is quoted as saying *Football is life.*

I pick up the book and thumb rapidly through it. There's Carter's basketball photo, Carter's baseball photo, Carter's senior photo. When I get to the index, I scan down to see *Wellesley, Carter: 7, 11, 29, 46, 52, 70, 112, 139, 150.*

He's in this book nine times. Jesus.

"Here, sign mine," Tracey says, sliding her yearbook across the table. I blink. I'm still a little amazed she knows my name, and now she wants me to sign it in her yearbook.

I flip to the fresh page in the back.

"Give me yours," she says, reaching out to snag my book.

I fish a pen out of the front pouch on my backpack

and then rest the tip on the page, but I don't know what to say. *I'm so glad we both hate Carter? Thanks for believing my lies?* Right. I listen to her own pen scratch across the page and so I just scribble down, *Tracey, hope you have a great summer. Sam Marshall.*

I push it back in front of her, but instead of giving me my book, she slides it over to Macy, who doesn't hesitate as she takes Tracey's pen and scribbles her own message into the back.

Then she gives me my book and her own, and I scribble down a derivative of what I've already said and hand it back.

I flip the yearbook open and glance at the back.

They both left their phone numbers. *Call me!* messages. Little hearts.

It makes my stomach hurt, seeing their positive, cutesy little notes.

Do they actually like me? Or is this still about Carter? Why can't I seem to believe they actually want to be friends with me?

I snap my yearbook shut and push it into my backpack, zipping it up. When I look up, Tracey and Macy are staring across the room, their backs rigid, their expressions identical.

I twist around in my chair and follow their gaze, my stomach sinking.

Carter just walked into the cafeteria with the guys who keyed my car. My breath leaves my lungs and I find my hands shaking as I grab at my backpack straps.

"Don't," Tracey says. "Don't give him the satisfaction."

The breath catches in my throat. "But I don't want—"

"Stay put. If he comes over here, we have your back."

Have my back? What does that even mean, really? That they'll play human shield if he launches himself at me, like he should? Like I deserve?

I dart my eyes over to him, and I find it hard to tear them away like I meant to.

He's different, now. He's not floating into the room like before, but walking, with sort of jerky, heavy-footed steps. Unless it's me that's changed. Unless I'm seeing him differently, seeing the guy he's always been.

But no, it's not just me. Where before, people used to part like the Red Sea, they're now ignoring him. He has to jostle his way through the crowd. He accidently bumps into someone's shoulder.

He's not the god he always was. Whatever I did, it stripped away the veneer of who he used to be. It made people see him for who he is. No, it made them see him for who he's *not*. Because they believe a complete and utter falsehood.

Now, he trips a little. No, wait. It kind of looked like someone purposely shoulder-checked him. He turns and glares, but the guy doesn't glance back, just keeps walking.

I don't know that guy. Why would he do that? Did he hear the rumor and choose my side without even knowing me?

A rumor can't be that powerful. *My* rumor can't be that powerful.

I can't seem to rip my gaze away from him. I'm riveted by watching his fall from grace, seeing the differences. His shoulders hunch forward a little, but his eyes are not downcast. They burn, even from here, with anger.

I gulp. "Guys, I really think—"

"No. Your butt stays in that chair," Tracey says. "And if you move, it'll only make him see you."

I see now why she is who she is. Why she reigns supreme amongst the girls, why they all listen to her. Because when she speaks, it's a command and everyone listens. I sigh, a shallow, shaky sort of sigh that only makes me feel more nervous.

"Okay," I say, though I'm not sure it really is.

I sink into my chair as Carter gets his yearbook. The line isn't very long any more, and he gets his book in minutes.

He tucks it under his arm, and his buddies follow him. He approaches a group of seniors, half girls, half guys. Couples, by the look of it, half of them draped all over each other. A few letterman jackets are mixed in, but some of the girls are wearing them. He pauses at the edge of the table, setting down his yearbook, pushing it toward the first guy.

I hold my breath. He signs it, passes it to the next guy.

The next guy, a redhead, pulls the book toward him, but the girl bumps his elbow and he drops it. There's a long, awkward pause, something I can see even from here. Carter stands there, fidgeting in a weird way as he stares at him. The guy doesn't look at him, because he's too busy looking at his girlfriend.

His perfect, blond, cheerleader girlfriend. I can see, even from here, that the girl is glaring at Carter, her eyes narrowed. Hard.

Slowly, glacially slowly, he pushes the yearbook to the next guy.

One at a time, they nudge it around the lineup until it's back in Carter's hands. None of them have signed it.

I feel sick as I watch him pick the book up. He hugs it to his chest, looking more vulnerable than I've ever seen. Looking smaller than I've ever seen. His shoulders, once so square, hunch over, and his chin, so high before, seems to curve into his chest.

I want to crawl under the table, curl up, and die there.

He's an ass. The biggest they ever made. But I didn't want to do this. I didn't want to be that girl, the one who blamed him, the one who created this punishment.

My dad always says, "What goes around comes around." He means, follow the rules and it all works out. He means that those who do whatever they want never prosper, that you reap what you sow. I don't think he means, "Be an asshole and some girl will accuse you of rape, and then people will believe it and life will really suck."

I sink further into my chair, except it's not really possible, because there's nowhere to go.

Carter twists around and glances back at the table as he walks away, heads toward the door, realizing he's not who he used to be. I can see it in him. I want to stand up, climb up on the table, tell them all they're wrong. Scream at them to stop punishing him.

And I don't.

Some twisted, angry part of me is happy I'm sinking into the seat, happy he's suffering right now, just like I did. Just like Tracey, Macy, the redheaded girl in the parking lot.

I'm mute, and I just sit there.

Carter pauses just shy of the door, twists again, and sees me.

His eyes burn into me. He stops, pauses. His feet stop moving and panic wells up in me. Something in his body shifts. He goes from dejected to determined.

Crap.

Crap.

Crap.

Crap.

Tracey and Macy move, and their chairs screech as they stand, Carter pushing toward us. His strides turn angry as he rushes toward me, as my stomach climbs into my throat and I think he might attack me. He's that angry right now, his eyes blazing.

But he doesn't get close enough for it.

A group of people seems to rise from nowhere, push toward him, surging in a big wave, a crowd—a group of people who seem to care about me when they shouldn't.

Carter doesn't make it anywhere close to me. The people become a wall, and his blond, tousled hair disappears. My mouth goes dry. The crowd shifts, and someone shoves

Carter. His face changes. And then he whirls around, stalking out, the door slamming behind him with a heavy thud.

And then they all turn and look at me.

Sixteen

If Veronica wasn't gripping my arm in a painful death grip, I would be in the parking lot right now, flying out of here. But I'm in the gym and she's dragging me up the bleachers. I can't seem to find a way to tell her I can't do this, not today.

I think she might actually be excited about this assembly. And somewhere, in the deep recesses of my brain, I remember a scene or two like this from freshman year. When Veronica was softer, more of an excitable, naïve girl than she is today. I feel a pang. I shouldn't have given up on her. We could have stayed friends. Instead I watched her drift away, and I didn't even attempt to get her back.

People watch us as we climb the stairs, past the cliques to which we don't belong. Just when I think she's going to continue to the very top row, she sits down in an empty spot. My eyes travel further up the bleachers, and I see a row of green and white letterman jackets. I spin around and plunk hard on the wooden bench, wishing I could sink into the bleachers, or even better, disappear underneath them.

Voices and footsteps echo against the ceiling in the cavernous gym. The basketball hoops have been cranked up, out of the way. Banners for our last few years of championships flutter silently against the walls. Half of those were teams Carter was on. Our new baseball championship banner has prime placement, right in the middle.

I watch in silence as the seats around us fill steadily from the stream of students entering the gym. I wonder if there's a neon sign flashing above my head, a giant arrow pointing down with the thousand names people must associate with me. *Liar. Slut. Victim.*

I start to feel warm, and wish I had worn something lighter than this long-sleeve V-neck.

I drop my eyes and stare at the buckle on the toe of my brown ballet flats.

"You cool?" Veronica's voice, soft in my ear, startles me.

I nod. "Uh-huh."

She reaches over and gives my hand a squeeze just as Mr. Paulson strides out to center-stage, a cordless microphone in his hand. He clears his throat into the thing and the loud roar dies into a low hum. "Welcome to the last assembly of the year!"

Cheers erupt. Summer is so close you can actually taste the watermelon, feel the cool water of Riffe Lake. I try to focus on that. All of this will just … disappear.

"You're all here today to celebrate another successful year at MHS! And tomorrow, our seniors will graduate!" His voice gets a comical, radio announcer boom for the last two words, but no one seems to care about how cheesy he sounds. Instead everyone begins the stomping and clapping that makes the entire stand of bleachers shake and rumble, filling the gym with a sound that would make a thunderclap proud.

"We will now introduce your senior athletes, the newest alumni of our storied Mossyrock High School sports program," Mr. Paulson declares. "Please welcome this year's senior varsity cheerleaders." He steps to the side as a blitzy pop beat bursts from the speakers. A small group of cheerleaders leap up from their spot on the bottom bleacher, forming a perfect V out on the floor through a series of cartwheels, leaps, and handsprings.

The song beats inside my lungs, but I'm not feeling the energy. I don't want to be here.

"Please welcome your retiring baseball team members! Starting with your captain, Carter Wellesley!"

He strolls down the bleachers, that familiar swagger now looking arrogant, and from this far away all I can do is imagine that cruel gleam in his eyes as they swept over my bare legs. He must be faking this confidence, though, because just two hours ago he looked so empty and alone.

What had been a loud, rumbling show of support turns...ugly. Behind me and below me, cheers erupt, but they're drowned out by something else.

Booing. It starts as a murmur, then becomes a low rumble that builds like thunder until it fills up the space. I glance around and see my classmates with their hands cupped around their mouths, booing with all they have.

Perfect, golden boy Carter, the one everyone loves to cheer, is being booed.

Carter steps onto the gym floor and his beaming, megawatt smile falters, turns tight and fake. The boos grow even louder as he makes it to the middle of the gym. His eyes are scanning the bleachers, looking for an answer to this but knowing he already has it.

The boos get louder. People twist around, looking for me in the stands. A few teachers stand up, make "cut it out" motions, try to get the booing to die down. Another teacher jumps up from the opposite bleachers and scurries over to the head cheerleader, saying something into her ear.

I feel my face grow hot as a bead of sweat trickles between my shoulder blades. I tug at the collar of my shirt.

Veronica leans in. "This is so awesome," she says under her breath. "Look at him. He doesn't even know what to do!"

The cheerleaders scramble to reverse it. One steps forward, grabs the mic from Mr. Paulson. "And your star center, Chad Biggins!"

The boos die out as Chad takes the floor, and Carter turns away and goes to make room for Chad. I see them lean in, whispering something. Plotting my demise, I'm sure.

"He finally knows what it's like. Three years, and he finally knows." Veronica says.

I raise a brow and look at her.

"Do you think he thought twice before telling everyone I was a lesbian? Do you think he even cared what it would do? It was at his house, you know. One of his parties, where he announced to everyone, 'Veronica Michaels is a muff diver.' He destroyed me, and now his own party is what got *him* in trouble. Rather fitting, don't you think?"

I purse my lips and shrug. How can she be so sure this is the right thing to do?

"Don't feel bad. After tomorrow he's going to escape all this. I wasn't allowed to do that."

I nod.

"Do you want to get out of here?"

I smile. "Yeah. That'd be awesome."

Seventeen

I follow Veronica through the door, two silver bells jingling as we step into the boutique clothing store, the only one in town. It's a tiny place, but the racks are packed.

Veronica picks up a crimson velvet jumper. "You should so wear this," she says.

"Moving on," I say, crossing the room. I nod at the sales girl, who is pulling a string of gum out of her mouth while flipping through a glossy magazine. "This is cute," I say, pulling out a peach-colored sleeveless shirt.

"Kind of. It's pretty plain, but I guess if you add accessories."

I nod and put it back on the rack, chewing on my

lower lip. "Hey Veronica?" I ask, twisting around. "Why are you being so nice to me?"

Veronica stares hard at the hanger in her hand, then looks up at me. "I don't know. I guess I feel guilty, sometimes, about leaving you behind."

"You didn't leave me behind," I say.

"Yeah, I did. I started hanging out with Miranda Rogers. You invited me over, and I told you I was hanging out with her, and you never called again."

"Oh."

She tips her head to the side. "Why didn't you ever try and call after that?"

What? "Why didn't *you*?"

She shrugs. "I was stupid, and I was having fun with Miranda, going to concerts and stuff. I kept thinking you'd call, and then before I knew it the school year was over, and it was summer, and we just never talked again."

Why am I sensing a trend? Why does it seem like everything I've ever lost was my own damn fault? Is it really that hard to fight for the things I want?

"It's been nice, you know. Talking again."

I nod. "Yeah, I know. I mean, I've liked it." I turn back to the rack. "How's your little sister? She must be what, nine now?"

"She just turned eleven. Already into makeup. My mom is terrified."

I laugh. Veronica smiles. "What's the deal with you and Nick these days? I've seen you holding his hand in the hallway."

I pull out a polka-dotted dress that turns out to be ugly and shove it back onto the rack. "Uh, I think we're kinda together. I think. We're going to the senior party together."

At least, we were. Maybe he doesn't want to go with me anymore. We haven't talked yet.

Her eyes flare wider. "I so should have bet on that. I saw it coming a mile away."

"Yeah?"

She nods.

My shoulders slump. "But if he finds out the Carter thing is a lie, there's no way he doesn't dump me."

"Hey. He won't find out. There's no reason for him to. Who's going to tell him?"

I shrug, with just one shoulder, not quite believing it. I pull out a pretty beaded dress, holding it up against my body. "I'm still not so sure about the whole thing," I say. "It doesn't feel right."

"Look, I know you're feeling bad about it, but don't. Carter did this to himself. Everyone would have ignored the rumor if he weren't such an asshole."

Two wrongs don't make a right, is all I can think. Another of my dad's stupid slogans.

But I don't say it.

"What do you think of this one?" I step away from the racks so that Veronica can get a better look.

"So pretty," she says. "You totally have to go try it on."

"Are you sure it wouldn't be better on you?" I thrust the dress at her.

She gives me a pointed look. "It's okay to be selfish once in a while, you know," she says, grinning.

"Oh, whatever," I say, sauntering away to the dressing room.

Inside, I shimmy out of my jeans. The stall next to me clicks open and shut. "Does it fit?" Veronica calls.

"I don't know yet," I say. "Did you find something?"

"Yep. It's a fringed flapper dress. Black."

Giggling. She's different here than she is at school.

"Can I ask you a question?" I ask, pulling my T-shirt over my head.

"Sure."

"Why'd you want to be one of them?"

She's quiet, and for a minute I doubt she heard me. Then, "I don't know. I just kind of fell into it. I mean, we were always sort of on the outskirts at school, and it always felt like people were judging me, and I guess I was just over it. I wanted to know what it was like on the other side."

I slide the shirt over my shoulders, twisting around to zip it up the side. "That's... very perceptive of you," I say, searching for the right words.

"Not really. Just spent a lot of time thinking about it. I'm kind of sick of it, to be honest."

"Really?" I step out of the stall and walk to the three-way mirror at the end of the dressing room. The silver beads glimmer from every angle, but only when the light hits them, so it's not garish or anything. Veronica comes out of her stall as well. "Yeah. I mean, I always thought being on the outside was harder. But once you're one of them … it's just a nonstop balancing act. She pauses. "That's amazing. I'm going to kill you if you don't get it."

I look in the mirror again. "Promise?"

"That I'll kill you?" she says, laughing.

"No, that it looks good."

"I mean it. Now put your regular clothes back on so that you can get it. I'm taking this one too. We'll be the best dressed girls at the senior party," she says, smiling.

"Okay, whatever you say."

I return to the dressing room, and for the first time, I'm looking forward to the party.

Eighteen

In the car on the way to graduation, it's unpleasantly silent. If I thought I could get away with it, I'd bail at a stop sign, run away, and never look back. Instead I just sink further into my seat, spreading the white robe out around me. I haven't spoken a word to my dad in twenty-four hours.

We're halfway to the ceremony before he finally breaks the silence. "I'm proud of you." He sits stiffly in the seat beside me as he pulls up at a stop light.

What? First he's screaming and now he's proud of me? "For?" I ask.

"Graduating," he says in a terse voice, giving me a look like that was a stupid question.

"Everyone graduates," I say, staring at my robe.

"But you have a great GPA," he adds gruffly. Pride isn't quite something he can pull off. It fits as well as an extra small T-shirt on his muscled frame.

All I can think is *too little, too late.*

Where was he ten years ago, when I wanted desperately for him to take me to the father-daughter dance because my classmates' dads were going? Where was he when I wanted to take ballet, and I showed up and was the only one in sweatpants, when I should have had a bun and a leotard and tights?

"Cut the crap, Dad."

"Excuse me?"

"My GPA is mediocre at best."

He narrows his eyes. "Which is why you should go to CCC, raise your GPA—"

"I'm not going to CCC!" I explode. I don't know if it's my dad or Nick or everything, but suddenly I can't be contained. "I told you this already! I want to be a writer. I want to go to UW and study English and do something for *me* for once."

His look hardens. "Why are you so angry?"

"Because—for once—I want a dad like everyone else has! A dad who supports me and is excited about me going to college! Instead I get the one who wants me to stay here forever!"

He blinks, then turns to look at me; he has the nerve to look as if I've hurt him. "I support you."

"You have a funny way of showing it." My voice comes out sharp and angry, spilling out in a way that's impossible to stop. Even *I'm* surprised by it.

My dad blinks. "Sam, I might not always show it—"

I can't take this. "*Might not always*? Give me a break, Dad! When do you *ever* show it? When do you show *anything*?! You're a freakin' machine or something. Do you know what it's like to grow up like that? Do you even care?"

My voice comes out as a high-octave screech. Maybe all the craziness as school has turned into something. Into … my ability to tell him the truth. Because a week ago, I went along with everything. I was perfect, obedient Sam. But I don't want to be that girl anymore.

He flinches.

I clench my jaw, hold onto my anger, will the hurt to stay walled up inside where it belongs. "Was Mom like you? Would she have been such a freakin' hard-ass all the time?"

He pulls back as if I slapped him. For a second, I feel bad about it. But I'm tired of feeling bad about everything, feeling guilty, feeling like everything is my fault.

He turns back to the road, blinks a few times but can't seem to answer. Instead he pulls over to the curb, underneath a big weeping willow. He shuts the engine off and we sit there, engulfed in the shade of the tree. I don't know why he pulled over, what he's thinking, but it can't be good. If I know anything, I know that conversations with Dad are never good.

For a long moment, I'm pissed off and I want to rip into him, but I can't seem to find the courage.

"You don't know her. You don't even really know who she was."

Wait … *what*?

"I was never supposed to do this alone."

My heart lurches. There's emotion in his voice. *Real* emotion … the tiniest tinge of vulnerability that cracks his perfect façade.

"You just … came out of nowhere," he says, with a sharp intake of air. I want to believe he's feeling something, something real, but it's nothing. It has to be nothing. My father is such a complete and total hard-ass.

It has to be nothing, I repeat again to myself.

"I would never undo any of this, but … I didn't know she would leave, and I'd be left figuring it all out, and doing a horrible job of raising you."

Silence engulfs us, confusion coursing through me. What can I possibly say to the man who has never shown me any vulnerability? It's all I can do to just breathe normally. I'll get choked up and he'll just sit there, steady as a rock, totally unaffected.

He sighs. "She wasn't like me. She was warm and funny and changed everything just by walking into a room. She had this way of making it seem like life was a game. Like … tomorrow wasn't a guarantee so we should all live for today."

He takes in a jagged breath of air. My own lungs burn. *Is* he upset about this? Why does he have to hide behind himself?

"All I ever wanted was for you to be different from her, *and* be like her at the same time," he says. "Everyone loved her, loved what she brought to life, and yet I would bet everything I have that she's unhappy even now, wherever she is. She's just one of those people that can never find satisfaction in anything. All I ever wanted for you was for you to understand that what we have… it's not so bad."

I blink hard against the tears that crop up from nowhere. My dad's voice is flat, gravelly. I won't give him emotion if he won't give it back. I clear my throat. "But you make me feel trapped here. In Mossyrock forever."

"You need to stay here. You're not mature enough to handle what's out there. You need to understand… what you and me have, it's not so bad."

"But how could I know that if I never learn anything different? If I stay inside this damned bubble you built for me?"

He turns to look at me, and I almost don't believe the mist in his eyes. He blinks and it's gone, and I know I imagined it. *Wanted* it. Wanted a dad who worried about me, was proud of me, was anything but a jerk.

"I know I'm doing this whole dad thing wrong, but I don't know any other way. Your mom took off six months after you were born. I guess I never did figure out just what the hell I was doing. And being in this job, it's too easy to figure the worst, and want to protect you from that, and harden yourself, and a thousand other things. I still don't know what the hell I'm doing. And now you're graduating."

I turn toward him. "It's not that difficult. All I ever wanted was for you to tell me you loved me. I wanted you to trust me. To let me be who I wanted to be. I wanted to not feel so alone all the time."

"I do love you," Dad says. "You're all I have. But you're also so much like her."

I close my eyes, rest my head on the seat and breathe deeply, trying to rein in the spiral of emotions. The hurt, the anger, the confusion. Dad never wants to talks about her, and all of the sudden he's spilling all of this. More than he ever did before. And he never says 'I love you,' and I hate myself for feeling something when he said it.

Everything swirls together and I just want out of this car. The air is hot and stifling and it's not enough.

"That's why you need to stay. That's why you need to understand my viewpoint. You're not ready."

His breathing is shallow, quick. I wonder, if I opened my eyes, whether I'd see actual emotion on his face.

"You're all I have left of her, and I don't know how I'd manage if something happened to you."

His voice cracks and I finally open my eyes, look at him, and the breath disappears from my lungs. His eyes are shimmering. Like maybe, in some alternate reality, he might actually shed a tear.

I can't look at him when he's like this, so different from the only dad I've ever known, so I look out the window.

It's starting to fog over from the cool spring air and the warmth of the car. I run a finger through the condensation.

"I'm trying to understand. I am. But I don't want to live in a box anymore," I say, my anger gone. "I'm *going* to UW."

He half sighs, half groans. "I won't let you."

"You have to."

"Do I?" he asks.

"Yes. I'm eighteen. If you don't give me your blessing, I'm going anyway."

He rolls to a stop at the stop sign, but doesn't move forward. I look in the rearview mirror, only half relieved no one is waiting behind us.

"I don't want you to go," he finally says, quietly.

I lean back in the seat. "I know. But I'm going."

"I don't think I can support that."

"I'm going either way," I say, my voice choked.

"So be it," he says.

Yes. So be it.

————

If it weren't for my dad's insistence, I wouldn't be here right now, standing in the corner of the room, hiding underneath this baggy white gown and silly cap, a gold tassel hanging down in my face. I keep looking for Carter, who would be in a green gown like the rest of the guys, but I haven't spotted him. Maybe he skipped the ceremony.

I find a chair and sit down against the wall, watching

forty-something kids from my senior class laugh and joke, excited to be taking the next step, nervous to be moving on, worried they'll miss all their friends.

I can't stop thinking about my dad, about how small he looked in the driver's seat. He hugged me when we got out of the car. I can't remember the last time he hugged me. It felt … weird. But kind of nice.

In the end, though, all I feel is a heavy sadness about it all, that the two of us have led such a long life of isolation when it didn't have to be that way. There's no resolution in this unsteady peace we've made. Just another jagged edge.

I glance at my watch, stare as the second hand ticks at least a hundred times. Nick and I still haven't talked. I don't know what he's thinking now. I feel more alone than ever as I search the crowd for him. I want to talk to him. I want to know we're okay. I want him to kiss me again.

He steps into the room just as someone else walks in and whistles. That's our cue to line up in alphabetical order. I'm in the middle with the other M's. Nick gives me a smile and a wave that sends relief flooding through me. It's so normal, like he's not mad at me at all. He ends up in line a dozen or so students in front of me.

I walk out, following the lineup, feeling as if I'm heading out to walk the plank, though I'm not sure why. Twenty-four hours from now, everything about school and my classmates will be behind me. Twenty-four hours.

I find my seat in the middle of the third row and settle into the creaking folding chair. I reach up to check my hair, patting the loose, salon-made curls I got this morning. I glance back just in time to see Carter dart out from the doors behind us, take the last empty seat near the back. He's sitting out of order. Trudy Xander and Paul Zimmerman should be after him.

He waited until the last moment to sit with his classmates.

Someone slides their chair away from him. Just a few inches, but it might as well be the Grand Canyon—the message it sends is just as harsh. Carter pretends not to notice, simply slumps into his chair and stares straight ahead.

I twist back around, look up at the parents and family members seated in rows that form a horseshoe around where the students sit. I try to find my dad, but his face is just one in a sea of a couple hundred, so I just twist back around and stare straight ahead, at the tassel dangling from the cap on the guy in front of me.

Mr. Paulson walks to the front and gives a dry, boring speech. He tells us that we'll gather our diplomas and then the valedictorian, a mousy girl I've shared a class or two with, will give her speech. Technically, she and Nick are both valedictorians, the only students in this school with a perfect 4.0 for four years running. But he's given plenty of speeches, and this will mean something to her.

It takes longer than it should, reading forty-five names. I wonder what it's like to go to high school with four hundred classmates instead of forty. I shift uncomfortably in my chair until my row is ready, then get up and follow the line until I'm the one standing at the podium, shaking the principal's hand as I accept my diploma.

A loud screeching whistle dwarfs the gentle clapping. I twist around to see my father. I recognize that whistle—he uses it all the time as a cop.

Unintentionally, I smile at him, feeling a tiny bit of the ice wall between us thaw. Then I turn and follow my classmates until I'm sitting in my chair again, and the rows behind me stand to take their turn walking down the aisle, student after student, flashbulb after flashbulb, cheers and clapping.

I'm leaning back against my folding chair, spacing out, when I hear, "Carter Wellesley."

I blink and look up, and the gentle, consistent clapping turns to a trickle, so that the loud cheering coming from his own family is obvious against the near silence. It's like screaming in the middle of an SAT session.

And then I know. The rumor has traveled beyond our high school. It's engulfed the town. If the adults know about it, how does my dad not know?

Carter grabs his diploma without shaking the principal's hand. Then another name is announced, and the clapping returns, and it's the difference between a bucket of water and the ocean.

I twist around to look at where the sounds of Carter's family came from, and I can see their heads ducked; they're whispering to each other, confused.

It must be his mom, with her golden-blond hair, and his sister and brother, both less than ten years old by the looks of it.

My stomach sinks.

Nineteen

I pivot in front of the mirror, staring down at my silver-beaded dress, adjusting my plain black headband. Everyone gets dressed up for these things, so it's not like I'm dressed strangely, but I'm nervous about being so ... *visible.* I'd convinced myself, while still in the store with Veronica pushing me, that I could pull it off.

But now it seems crazy bold. Shiny, shimmery, completely not me. I've got on matching silver, strappy heels I borrowed from Veronica. They rub the back of my feet a little. They're only an inch and a half high, but I've never really worn heels before, except for that disastrous night with Carter.

My hair hasn't changed since the graduation ceremony ended twenty minutes ago, but it looks nicer with the glittery beaded dress.

I chew on my lip and stare down at my silhouette, glad none of my classmates have wandered into the bathroom. Nick is waiting for me, I know that, but I find it hard to leave the bathroom. I suppose I look good. And if Nick and I were together like this without the secret hanging over me, I'd feel happy. Maybe excited, like I was on the verge of something other than tears.

Instead I'm standing here knowing how many pairs of eyes are going to stare me down. How many people are going to be watching me, waiting for me to fall to pieces because supposedly, just a week ago, Carter went too far.

If I so much as trip, I'm screwed.

This could have been different. I never had to act like I was going after Carter in the first place. Nick kissed me at the humane society because he *wanted* to; Reyna dumped him because he couldn't stop talking about *me*. If I'd thought things through—if I had, just once, put myself out there—maybe we could have been something.

But school's over. Graduation is done. This is the last time I really have to see any of my classmates. It worked out just like Tracey and Macy said. Everyone believed the lie, believed everything. Carter "got what he deserved," and next week he leaves for California.

It tastes bitter, this victory. Like I sucked on a rotten lemon, and now it's ruined me for everything else. I got away with it. Carter's been punished, and everyone believes me.

But I don't want it any more. I have everything I thought I wanted, but it's no longer worth the price.

I'm going to tell Nick, tonight. He'll be the first one. And then somehow I'll tell everyone else. I can't keep lying to him. I can't keep *destroying* Carter. He maybe an asshole. He may be a lot of things. But he's not a rapist.

Somehow I'll make everyone believe, everyone *know* the truth.

I get back up and look at myself in the mirror again. I twist my mouth to the side and fight the urge to pick at my hair, then leave the bathroom. My shoes clack across the cement, until I round the corner and see Nick leaning against his Mustang.

He's decked out in a crisp blue jeans and a new, deep blue button-up, a ball cap sitting crooked on his head. He smiles and it's impossible not to smile right back at him. "You look amazing," he says, his eyes sweeping over me.

"Thanks. You look pretty good yourself."

It's crazy, to think I'm really going to the senior party with him, my best friend all these years. I hate that it took all this for us to finally get together, that we lost those three or four years we could have been something.

And I'll miss the next few years after he learns what really happened. It'll probably take that long for him to forgive me. But I can't live with myself otherwise. Everything will turn into a pumpkin at midnight, but for now, I can pretend I'm really the girl at the ball, the girl whose true love might just love her back.

Nick opens the car door with a flourish, a cheesy, overacting sort of sweep of his arm that makes me giggle, and a piece of me unwinds.

"Your carriage awaits," he says.

I think I'm going to roll my eyes, but I don't, because somehow I find the whole stupid thing charming. I have hours until I plan to tell him, so I may as well enjoy them.

I sink into the seat, smoothing out the beaded dress, somewhat anxiously crossing my ankles, which is kind of silly because ... it's *Nick*. But being dressed up like this, and knowing that this may be my last night with him if he doesn't react well to the truth ...

"You should dress like that more often," he says.

I snort. "Like I'm going out on the town? When there's nowhere in this town to go?"

"Well, no, not like that. Just ... with your hair done up and makeup and all that."

I shoot him a skeptical look.

"I don't mean all decked out. I just mean ... you're always burying yourself in sweatshirts and sunglasses. It's nice to see you just embrace it."

"Embrace what? Freezing my ass off?"

"I was going with your natural beauty, but whatever."

I giggle nervously. Natural beauty. I don't know if I believe him, but I like hearing those words spoken about me. "You're such a nerd."

"That's why you love me," he says.

I snort and it turns into an odd cough, and soon enough I'm wracking my lungs. That's the third time he's said it this week.

He smiles back at me, and then I know he knows, and my cheeks flush. I turn to look out the window as he backs out of his parking space.

———————

We drive north, silence falling around us as we head toward a pier in Olympia. The parking lot that stretches along the road is mostly full as we glide into one of the last available spaces. Nick puts it in park and we sit in silence for a long moment, staring out at the glittering water in front of us, the city lights reflecting on the dark water.

"You okay? You've been kind of quiet."

His tentative tone makes my heart clench. He's saying it like he's worried about me, like I'm still grappling with a supposed rape.

I guess people are right. Maybe the truth really would set me free. It doesn't make it easier to say it, though. I turn to him and smile, hoping it reaches my eyes. "Yeah. I'm just ready to put all this behind me."

He reaches over and squeezes my hand and then tells me to sit tight as he walks around the back of the car. He opens my door, reaches out to grasp my hand, and pulls me to my feet. I smooth out the beads on my dress as I stand, then cross my arms at my chest. It's colder here, on the water. The spring night air has given way to a gentle, salty breeze coming off Puget Sound.

I take Nick's arm as he leads me across the uneven pavement, up to the big ramp that leads to the boat rented for the occasion. We all had to pay a hundred bucks for tickets, but it's a tradition—an eight-hour party that lasts until four a.m. We're not allowed to know anything else about the party ahead of time, or what, exactly, we paid a hundred dollars for.

We climb up the ramp, my hand gliding across the cool iron railing until we're on the deck of the boat. Sparkling white Christmas lights zigzag back and forth over the deck, creating a canopy we walk under as we make our way to the propped-open double doors.

There's an enormous ballroom inside. Swing music plays in the background as a disco ball sends sparkling lights splashing across the walls. Throngs of people, mingling in clusters, are sprinkled on the dance floor. A few tables span from one side of the room to the other, and waiters are busy bringing out trays of food. The opposite wall has dozens of round tables, covered in green felt, with men and women in black button-downs standing on one side, dealing cards. We pause in the doorway as I take it all in.

"It's a casino night," Nick says. "Cool."

I nod, staring across the open expanse at the crowds laughing and talking. The hum of their voices grows louder. It's as important as spring break and senior skip day.

"Let's go sign in and see how this works."

We move further into the room and I pull my gauzy shawl closer, as if to protect myself from the looks of my classmates. I follow Nick to the long table closest to the door, and he leans in and gives our names. The red-headed woman, one of two math teachers at MHS, reaches under the table and pulls out two small plastic baskets. "These are your chips. Gamble them any way you like. At the end of the night, you can cash them in for prizes."

"Got it," Nick says, handing me my chips.

We push our way through the crowd, Nick holding my fingers so we don't get separated. Finally, we emerge into a clearing near the disco ball. Yellow light splashes across the floor beneath our feet.

"Let's dance," Nick says, his voice close to my ear.

"No one is dancing," I say, darting a look at the empty floor, white lights from the disco ball glimmering across the hardwoods.

"So?"

"So everyone will stare. And you're a terrible dancer."

"I'll pretend not to be insulted. Also, everyone will stare at you anyway. So let's give them something to look at." He pauses. "Even if it's just me making an idiot of myself."

"What do I do with these?" I ask, holding the chips up.

"They're called pockets." Nick takes the chips from my hand and shoves them into his pocket, then drops his own into the opposite pocket. His jeans bulge with the chips and it looks ridiculous, but he just smiles at me in that genuine way of his.

I swallow and look at up him, finding myself nodding even though I hadn't planned on it.

He interlaces his fingers with mine and pulls me across the floor, and we dodge the clusters of our classmates until we're standing in the empty expanse under the disco ball. Some of them turn to look at me, to watch me, but I ignore them until we're facing each other and I don't have to look at anyone but Nick.

The swing song bleeds into something slower, something we can both manage. And then he's reaching for my other hand and placing them both over his shoulders, and his hands are on my waist as the song seems to grow a little louder and the whispers seem grow quieter.

I let him pull me close enough that I can lean into him and close my eyes and concentrate on the swaying of our bodies. The whispers die out completely and I am glad, in this moment, that I'm here. I'm liking this. The first normal thing that's happened in a week. I guess it's a blessing the senior party goes all night. Maybe it will never end.

Minutes pass and I keep my eyes shut, so I'm surprised when I open them to find that the floor has filled in. A dozen couples are dotting the floor around us and I recognize Tracey, Macy, and Veronica among them. They smile at me and nod as they sway with their partners, and I smile back.

"See? Not so bad, right?" Nick gives my back a squeeze and I nod.

"No, not so bad at all."

The song switches and the beat kicks up a notch. "Do you want to keep dancing or go get something to drink?" Nick asks.

I pull away. "A drink would be good."

He pulls me back through the crowd, which has continued to thicken. It might just be me, but I swear the stares aren't as intense as they were before. Does it only take a week to get tired of a rape rumor? Are they over it already, moving on to the next big thing?

A few people I've never talked to outside of school smile and nod at me. Even a football player. I grip Nick's hand tighter as we have to bump into a few people to make it through.

Soon we're standing next to a few big troughs of ice. "Pepsi okay?"

I nod and take the sweating, icy can from his grip and pop the top.

"What next?"

I look over at the cluster of tables. "Let's go try our hand at poker," I say. "I kind of want to sit down. These heels are killing me already."

He laughs. "I have to admit, they're kind of hot, but I'm not sure you're the high heels type."

I smile, feel a blush warm my cheeks. "I'm not. Hence, they're killing me."

"Say no more," he says, leading me once again by the hand. Maybe it's silly, but it does make me feel a little less...lost.

We cross the crowded room and I feel my confidence growing, like I can handle anything anyone dishes up. Like tonight can go okay, and I can tell the truth, and things won't fall apart.

We take a seat on the stools near one of the poker tables. Now that we're sitting, I notice that the once barely discernible rocking of the boat has taken on a graceful, slow sway. We must have pushed away from the dock. I twist and look out the huge tinted windows as the spar-kling shoreline creeps away.

The dealer, a twenty-something guy with close-cropped blond hair, explains the game and asks for a por-tion of our chips. I take out five blue ones from the plastic tray and stack them on the felt in front of me.

Even with the rules, I'm not sure what I'm doing. I get a Jack, a Two, a Five, a Three, and a Seven. I plunk them all down but the Jack. "Uh, I'll take four."

He slides four cards my way. Nick asks for one, and gets a replacement.

I have two Jacks. Somehow that means I win, and I get an extra chip for my efforts.

Nick sets his chips down. "I need to use the restroom. Will you be okay for a little bit?"

I nod.

"You sure?"

"Yes, I can survive for five minutes. Go," I say, waving my hand. "But I'm so using your chips if I run out before you get back."

He pushes back from the table and disappears into the crowd. I turn back to the felt and ask for another hand, putting a chip down.

I play a couple of rounds, but there's no sign of Nick. My classmates filter in my direction, littering the tables around me. I pull at the beading on my dress, nerves creep-ing back in. After another hand, I take my remaining chips and stand, a little wobbly on my heels, moving through the crowd in search of Nick. I brush by my classmates, nod and smile. A redhead, Britney, eyes me with interest, but everyone else just smiles warmly and turns back to their group.

There's a garbage can along the back wall so I head that direction, hoping to ditch my empty Pepsi can. I drop it into the garbage and turn to head toward the bathrooms, when I collide with someone. My chips clatter loudly to the ground.

Furious blue eyes glare down at me. My mouth goes dry all at once.

Carter.

"I—"

"Shut up. Just *shut up*," he growls.

The hairs on my arms stand on end at the tone of his voice, the absolute venom lacing his words.

My eyes sweep over his face, take in the dark shadows under his eyes. He looms closer, and then I realize they're not shadows at all. His left eye, normally a sparkling blue, looks a little bloodshot and has a dark, black circle underneath. His cheek is so swollen he looks like a chipmunk, and his bottom lip is split, crusted with fresh blood. Did he go to the ceremony like this? Or did it happen here?

Everything inside me deflates. He looks nothing like the perfect golden god he was a week ago.

"You did this to me, and I want to know why," he says, in a low, furious tone.

On purpose or not—it doesn't really matter, does it? I *did* do this to him.

"I got jumped because of you," he says, spitting the words. "Because of your *lies*."

I try to form words, but it seems impossible with him this close to my face. It's hard to just breathe—forget speaking. There's at least a foot of air between us, but it feels like there's nothing, like he's sucking the oxygen right out of my lungs, pushing down on my rib cage.

I dart a look around, but we're standing behind a poster perched on an easel and no one has noticed us. "Carter—"

"Why the *fuck* did you have to do this? Huh? Just for spite? Because I didn't want you?"

Desperate to breathe, I take in a ragged breath of air, but it does nothing to stop the pain in my chest.

I want to tell him. Everything. Tell him I'm sorry for what I did, more sorry than he could ever, in a million years, know. Tell him I never meant for this to happen— that I hadn't run out and created the lie, that I'd just stood by and watched it spin out of control.

Tell him that I deserve whatever he wants to do to me.

"Why? WHY did you have to ruin me?" His voice cracks, and I shatter.

He's not as strong as I thought he was. His unwavering, solid front gives way to the pain I've caused him, and it's enough to make my knees buckle. I have to put my hand out against the wall to steady myself.

I am dirt. Lower than low. This boy is broken, and I did it, and somehow I justified it, and it's wrong. More wrong than I could have imagined.

"My *parents* heard about this. They wanted to know why I was booed at graduation. My own mom looked at me like ... like ... ARGH!" He runs his hands through his hair and for a second, I think he's going to actually rip it out. He turns away and his chest heaves and he looks back at me, so broken and so angry all at once.

My lip trembles. "Carter, I'm—"

"No," he says, anger winning. "You've talked enough. It's *my* turn."

I swallow hard against the boulder in my throat, but it's no use. I feel as if I'm choking.

"Everyone believes you. Everyone thinks I really did it."

"I didn't start the rumor!" I blurt out. "I swear—"

"I'm not a rapist," he says, his voice nearly a growl. "Everyone thinks I am and I'm not." He grinds his teeth. "I don't understand how you could do this to me." His voice has bounced back to hurt. Now he sounds empty, like a little boy. Is he this conflicted, this much of a mess? He pulls back, and for the first time, there's more than a foot between us. I take in a big swallow of air, trying to bring myself together, trying to make him understand that somehow, I'll fix this. Somehow, everyone will know the truth.

Just as I open my mouth to say something, a fist flies.

At Carter. I stand in shock as Carter crumples to the ground and Nick rushes forward, throws his arms around me, and drags me close. I blink against the light.

"Are you okay?" His warmth seems to wrap around me all at once and I should feel safe, but I don't. I feel sick. "Sam, I ... God, I'm so sorry. I shouldn't have left you. I didn't know he was here, or I wouldn't have left you alone."

Carter moans somewhere near our feet. Dread fills me

up like a giant sandbag, getting heavier and heavier until I want nothing more than to sink to the floor.

"I can't believe … God, are you okay?"

The tears brim, roll down my cheeks. I hate myself more than anything in the world right now, as Nick's arms tighten around me and I see a few guys from the baseball team appear around us, helping Carter to his feet.

I want to bury my face in Nick's button-down and let it all out, tell him everything, start to finish, like I should have to begin with.

I wriggle around, place my hands against Nick's chest. I push, needing some air, enough distance to tell him the truth. He's caught off-guard and loosens his arms, and a gap widens between us. My eyes shimmer as I meet his, studying the deep blue, the yellow flecks near the pupil. Because when I open my mouth, when I tell him the truth, I'll probably never get this close again.

I'm done with this. I'm done with all of this. I've ruined both Carter's life and my own with one little lie. Maybe I never meant to tell it—maybe I'm not the one who spread it to begin with—but I had the chance to stop it all and I didn't. I let myself get swept up in it. I made choice after choice that condemned Carter. *I* gave him the split lip, the black eye, the swollen cheek. *I* ruined him, a little more every day.

I try to clear my throat but there's a giant, sandy rock jammed in there. I try again. "Nick—

"Sam!" Someone is hollering my name. I turn and it's

Veronica, Macy, and Tracey, pushing through the crowd to get to me.

I shake my head at them, and Veronica's expression changes. She glances at Carter and then back at Tracey and Macy. Tracey's lips part and she starts to step forward, and I know by her expression she wants to stop me from doing what I'm about to do. But I put up a hand and she freezes, and then I turn back to Nick.

I sniffle and look at the crowd gathering around me, at Nick's confused blue eyes, and at Carter's narrowed ones as he holds a hand to his soon-to-bruise cheek.

I clear my throat, and then in loud, carefully articulated words, say, "I lied."

No one moves. No one even breathes. I swallow, raise my voice. "Carter didn't do it."

The expression on Nick's face slices straight through me. It's disgust, disappointment, shock.

Veronica stands there, eyes shining, as if in awe. There's a strange sense of power that washes over me as I look at her.

I'm doing the right thing.

I turn back to look at the growing crowd. "I went into his room that night. But I was drunk—" I stop. I don't need to place any of the blame on Carter. I don't need to tell them what he said in that room. "And I tripped, hit my face on his dresser, and ripped my top." I clear my throat again. "When he left his room and I followed him, I think I was crying. Somebody took one look at me sobbing, and saw my bruised cheek and torn shirt, and jumped to conclusions."

Tears roll unbidden down my cheeks now, as I stand there alone, the circle of students not crossing the invisible barrier. I better get used to it, I suppose.

Nick looks like he's playing freeze tag—he's not moving, not blinking, not anything. I feel like an actor in a Shakespearean play, giving my monologue to a shocked, captivated audience.

This one is definitely a tragedy.

"I had no idea what everyone thought had happened until halfway through Monday. It just…spiraled out of control."

I scan the crowd, and see a spot where one person has separated from the rest.

"I'm sorry, Carter. I know *sorry* isn't enough to make it up to you, but I am."

A sob escapes my throat, racks my shoulders, but I try desperately to stand tall, my cheeks burning hot. I turn to look at Nick, who's standing in front of me, disgust on his face. I lower my voice, stare into his eyes. "I never wanted this. Any of this."

"But you lied to *me*," he says, his own fury rising to match Carter's just moments ago. "You're my best friend and you lied to me."

"Because you never asked me!" My voice screeches. "You stormed into my house and decided you knew the truth."

"It *was* the truth!" he says, throwing his hands up in

the air. "I knew it didn't make sense. I knew it hadn't happened. I was right!"

"I know. I just didn't know what to do because you stormed in so angry, and you only asked if I had lied, and I hadn't. Not then—because I never said he did this. I didn't start the rumor."

My voice cracks. "You don't understand. I never meant for this to happen. I never created this lie."

He visibly blanches, takes a step back, wrenches his look away from me and looks back at Carter—who now has a second black eye to match the first. It's swelling rapidly, and I can barely make out one of his blue eyes.

And then Nick shakes his head and looks back at me. "It doesn't matter. I don't trust you."

My nose is snot-filled and my throat aches. "I know."

Whatever we had, whatever we *could* have had … it's over.

My heart has shattered, hollowed me out inside. I'm in love with Nick and now I can never have him, because he'll never forgive me. The gentle kisses, the playful hairtugs, the stupid jokes—it's all over, and I've lost him.

We stare at one another for a long stretch of a moment. It goes on for eternity, as his eyes bore into mine and I try to memorize the way he looks right now, this close to me. Because after this … he's never going to look at me again.

I'm wearing a scarlet letter, but this one is for *liar*.

————

I stumble across the deck, pulling my shawl tighter around my shoulders as my tears shimmer. I find a place near the railings and sit, my legs stretched out in front of me, crossed at the ankles.

And then I lean back and stare out across the midnight-dark water, some part of me wishing I could just jump in and watch the boat steam away without me.

I played with fire, waiting so long to tell the truth, and I got burned. I never should have let Veronica, Macy and Tracey talk me into keeping the lie. I never should have let Nick think it happened.

I never should have ruined Carter's life like this.

That's what it really boils down to, in the end. Not me. I ruined Carter.

I ruined *him*. It wasn't Michelle, who started the rumor, or Nick, who freaked out on me, or Tracey, Macy, and Veronica, who talked me into keeping it. It was me.

I sigh and lean my head against the railing, my eyes shut, as I feel the boat beneath me bob gently on the waves. A week was all it took to tear apart everything. Eighteen years living in this godforsaken town, and a week to tear it all down.

I hear the clicking sound of shoes crossing the deck, and I open my eyes to see Veronica smiling tentatively down at me. "Room for me to sit?"

I blow out a breath of air. "Yeah, go ahead. But I don't know if you'll want to be associated with me after this."

She plunks down near the next railing post, stretching

her feet out so that ours nearly touch. For a moment, we just listen to the water slapping the side of the boat. "I'm sorry."

I blink. "What do you have to be sorry for? This is my mess."

"Maybe. But I feel like a bit of an idiot, leading the brigade against Carter. You didn't like it from the start. And it's obviously just made things harder for you."

The breeze off the water ruffles my bangs. "I could have said no. I could have told the truth. I had a hundred opportunities to tell the truth, and I chose not to. I went along with your plan because it was the easiest way to avoid the problem."

She nods, but doesn't speak. Moments pass, and I pull at the beads on my dress.

She looks up at me. "It's kind of hard to believe this is almost over, you know? So many of us are going to leave Mossyrock."

"There's no reason to stay."

She nods. "I know. I guess that's the point, really. There's nothing for anyone in our town. But people still stay."

I nod. "Yeah. I'm ready to move on, though."

"You think?"

I'm not surprised she's surprised. Maybe she thought I'd be one to stay forever.

"Yeah. Maybe a week ago, I wouldn't have been. I mean, I had all the paperwork ready, but *I* wasn't ready. But now, with everything... I don't know. I'm ready to go somewhere, be someone. Make choices that are my own, for once."

"Where are you headed?"

"UW. You?"

"UCLA," she says.

I nod, staring out at the water.

"It'll be weird, going somewhere where no one knows you," she says.

"I think I need that. To just start over and be someone else. I want to try some new things, you know? Branch out."

She nods. "Me too. I'm ready for a whole new reputation."

I laugh, a quiet, under-my-breath sort of laugh. She's not the only one. "It's been nice, you know. Having you back."

She nods. "Yeah. You too. Kind of sucks that we had to have something so stupid happen in order to talk to each other again. Don't be a stranger, okay?" She's climbing to her feet, one hand on the railing.

"Yeah, sure."

She glances at her watch. "You going to sit out here for the next five hours?"

I smile. "Yeah, I think so."

She pulls off her little jacket. "Then at least take this."

I want to object, but a shiver trembles through me and so I just smile and pull on the jacket. "Thank you."

"Any time. You sure you're really okay out here?"

"Yeah," I say, sighing. "I will be. Eventually."

"Okay. See ya," she says, walking back to the party, her arms crossed at her chest.

A breeze kicks up again and I pull Veronica's jacket tighter around me. Behind me, as she opens the door, the sounds of a piano melody float out to me, before fading.

————

Hours later, the boat slows, approaching the docks. I blink and readjust the way I'm sitting because my legs are numb. It may be June, but the water has cooled the night air and it's like I'm slowly freezing.

The boat glides to a stop and I sigh. The night is over, and I'm definitely not Cinderella anymore. My carriage is a pumpkin and my dress has turned to tatters, and the prince knows I'm a peasant. I want nothing more than to find my way home to my warm bed, climb in, and turn off the lights and hope the world outside just goes away.

I get to my feet, giving one last lingering look out across the water. I'm going to have to call my dad, now. And explain why he has to drive sixty minutes to pick me up.

"You have a cell phone, right?" I spin around to see Nick standing there, his hands shoved into his jean pockets, a cold look on his face.

"You're talking to me?"

"What you've done is seriously *fucked up*," he says. "I am *not* talking to you. Do you have your phone?"

I gulp. Nick doesn't cuss. Like, ever. I nod.

"Good. Find your own way home."

He turns around and walks purposefully across the deck of the boat, and I scurry after him. "Nick!"

"What?" he barks, whirling around. "You think you have the right to expect something?"

I stop, blinking.

"Well, no, but—"

"Just don't. Don't even think about it."

He twists around and strides away, and it's all I can do to keep up in these stupid little heels that pinch my toes and rub my ankle.

I follow him to his car, desperate for him to turn around, to just listen to me. His car sits in darkened shadows in the quickly emptying parking lot. He slinks to the Mustang and slams the door. I blink, hard, against the tears. For a long second I stand there, shivering, feeling as if the door slammed in my face. When he fires it up and the deep exhaust rumbles through the silence, I finally scurry after him, heels scraping along the broken concrete, and then yank open his door.

"Stop! Please, just stop."

He doesn't look at me, but he doesn't yank the door closed either. All I can do is hope it means something.

"I'm sorry," I say, desperation leaking into my voice.

He grinds his teeth, his eyes narrowed in an expression I barely recognize.

I sniffle. "Are you never going to talk to me again?"

He doesn't speak, just squeezes the wheel harder.

"Nick?" I chew on my lip, begging him with my eyes

to just *look at me*, as my fingers grip the cool metal of his car door. "Please?"

He twists around and gives me a look that freezes my heart. It's pain, and anger, and betrayal, and a thousand things mingled together.

"How? Huh? *How* could you do that to him? To me?" He tears his eyes away and looks out the windshield again, his jaw set.

I open my mouth and snap it shut. "I don't know," I finally say.

He lets out an angry, bitter bark of laughter. "You ruined his life and you don't know how you were able to do it?"

I look down, at the dirty concrete beneath my heels. "No. I do. I didn't start the rumor, but I kept it going because it was easier."

He shakes his head. "You're unbelievable, you know that?" He glances over with a look that slices through me. "It was easy to lie to me? To let me believe someone *raped* the only girl I've ever really loved? Do you know how many times I wanted to fucking kill him for what I thought he did?"

My lip trembles. "I'd give anything to undo it all."

"I guess it's too bad that you can't, then, huh?" he says, furiously.

"Do you hate me?"

He throws his hands up in the air. "No, Sam, I *love* you. But you know what? I'm not sure I really like you all that much."

I swallow, because it's the only thing I can manage, and turn back to the brightening skyline, trying desperately not to cry and mostly failing. Tears slide silently down my cheeks. Time passes in stifling, suffocating silence while Nick stares straight ahead, refusing to even glance my way. Finally, he reaches out and unpeels my fingers from his car door before slamming it shut and backing his car out of the parking spot.

Then I sit down on the curb and cry, texting my father while wiping the tears from my cheeks.

———————

Although it should take my dad over an hour to arrive, he pulls up in approximately five whole minutes. I furrow my brow and stare as his Charger crosses the lot, the tires squealing. Before I can stand up from my space on the cold concrete curb, he's out of his car, striding across the lot so fast I want to jump up and flee.

"What the hell has been happening to you?"

I feel the blood drain from my face as I stand, staring back at my dad as he turns red, whirls around, and paces a second before coming right back to me. "I've been circling this goddamn parking lot for two hours, fuming. I talked to Nick's mother hours ago because she heard an … interesting story from the neighbor."

I sink back to the curb and bury my face in my knees. Oh. That kind of story.

"How could you not tell me?" he asks, his voice rising.

And it's not even all anger, like it normally is. There's fear laced into it. "How could you let me hear this from someone else?"

Of course. Yet another thing I should have done, another way this all went wrong. I should have realized my dad would hear of this.

"It didn't happen," I say.

"What?" he says, bounding over.

"It didn't happen," I repeat, raising my face to look at him. His expression is frozen somewhere between relief and fear. "It was a lie. Not mine ... " My voice trails off. "No, yes. I lied. People thought that it happened, and I didn't tell them no, so it's my lie, but it didn't happen. Not really."

My father is like a balloon deflating. At once, he's sinking onto the curb beside me, leaning into me, breathing deeply. For the first time in a long time, I feel the heat of his body against mine, can smell the Old Spice scent of him. "So you're okay," he says.

"Mostly," I reply, but my voice sounds so sad and empty. "Physically, anyways. I screwed up some things. But that ... what you heard ... it didn't happen."

He heaves the biggest sigh I've ever heard, and for a second, it almost makes me feel warm, wanted, appreciated. I think he might just lie down on the concrete in some kind of weird euphoric daze. I stare up at the twinkling stars for a long moment, listening to my father's laborious breathing.

"Thank God," he finally says.

I don't know why, but I giggle. I shake my head, knowing everything is over and gone, but still, I giggle. I've lost everything and in the end my dad is so relieved, it's comical.

"I don't know what I would have done if it was true," he says, his voice quiet, solemn, so different from his normal voice. "Other than shoot him."

I put a hand up to silence him. The lines in his face seem deeper than they did just a few hours ago. I open my mouth, as if to refute what he said, but I find myself just sitting there. So instead I say, "It's not true. But it *is* a long story."

I scrunch over and bury my face in my knees, inhaling the scent of our laundry detergent, the only comforting thing I can think of right now.

Then I sit up and stare into my father's eyes. For the first time in a very long time, they're concerned, solemn, and he's ready to *listen* instead of dictate.

"It started a week ago ... "

Twenty

I'm sitting on the edge of my bed, staring across the yard into Nick's room. The curtains are wide open, fluttering in the warm late-July breeze. The walls of Nick's room are shockingly bare, and even his small flat-screen is gone. There's just one box left on his bed, and I watch as Nick steps into his room to retrieve it. I knew he was leaving for the East Coast early, to settle in, find a part-time job and all that, but I wasn't prepared for this day to come so soon.

I lean forward, an elbow on my windowsill, begging him to turn and look at me. *Begging* him to remember who I am, to care, even the tiniest bit, about how I'm doing.

To somehow find the forgiveness he's brushed aside. The forgiveness I don't deserve.

I miss him. So fiercely it hurts.

Four weeks of silence. I've texted him, emailed him, and called him, and he refuses to speak to me. My voicemails are pathetic, pleading, tear-filled, but it never matters, because what I did isn't forgivable. The silence is what I deserve. But it still aches, a bone-deep sort of pain that never leaves, haunts me, follows me everywhere I go. He's been my best friend for over a decade, and now I'm alone.

I stare across the expanse of yard, into the bedroom I always wished was mine, as Nick bends to pick up the box and catches me staring.

The moment is caught somewhere, suspended. He stops, and my heart picks up to a gallop as he stares back, meeting my eyes for the first time in weeks. The seconds stretch on and my heart climbs into my throat, hope swelling in my chest. He hasn't so much as acknowledged my existence for the last month. And now, for the first time, he's looking right at me.

I try to smile. I attempt to, but I don't know that it's real, that it matters, because it feels awkward—stiff and unnatural. I don't even know if smiling is okay with him, is okay with *me*. Is it normal, or acceptable, to be smiling and pretending I deserve him, given everything that's happened?

He walks to his window and I sit up straighter, gripping the windowsill, still smiling softly, timidly at him.

Then he pulls the drapes shut.

Everything inside me plummets to my feet, and tears spring to my eyes as I realized he's rejected me yet again.

I lie back on my bed and, moments later, I hear his car fire to life. I listen with a hollowed-out feeling as he shifts into gear. I strain to hear any hint of his car turning around ... until the sounds of it die away, the last time I'll ever hear that car of his.

He didn't even say goodbye.

Twenty-one

I wander down the aisle of Mossyrock grocery, my ballet flats shuffling across the ugly tiles as overly bright
fluorescent lights shine down. My eyes roam the packages
stacked six feet high, and then I turn back to my shopping list. I feel lost inside this store, a store I've shopped
in all my life. It's amazing how quickly you can forget the
most basic things, how easy it is to distance yourself from
another world, another life. A *previous* life.

I pass the seasoning packets and pause, plucking two
packages of brown gravy from the shelf.

I don't like gravy, but my dad does. So does his new
girlfriend.

Girlfriend. The mere thought of it sends simultaneous butterflies and uncertainty through me. I can't remember my dad ever having a girlfriend, and I definitely can't remember him ever saying such puke-worthy, cutesy things about how wonderful a woman is. He's never done *that.* She's the new town clerk or something. I haven't met her yet, and part of me wants to beg off, go back to my dorm, pretend it's not Thanksgiving weekend. I could eat at the cafeteria for the next four days. Catch up on homework and marathons of *The Real World.*

I could work on my book. It's halfway done. Sometime after graduation, my writer's block broke. I found my voice again. The story's not a romance, now. It's dark and twisting, unfurling as I write it. Unlike all those cheesy romance novels I wrote before, this one doesn't have a foregone conclusion, doesn't know what it will become. I filled an entire notebook, and still I write, and still it pours out.

But... it's different than before. I haven't shared the whole book yet, because it's not ready, but I've shared a few pieces. Instead of hiding the books under my bed, I joined a writer's club. We get together once a week in a coffee shop and write. It's total crap, and I know it's crap, but...

It feels good. Therapeutic, kinda. I lost everything for the lie. I *deserved* to lose everything. But somehow I'm rebuilding. Somehow, I'm finding myself amidst the shattered pieces.

I toss the packets into my handbasket and then turn to go find the sour cream, but I've hardly gone three steps before I look up and see the face that sends my heart plummeting into my feet.

The two of us freeze—stand six feet apart and simply stare. I take in a sharp breath of air, feel the overwhelming urge to ditch my basket and bolt, but I don't.

Instead I stare back at Carter.

He looks good. He looks like he used to... warm, tanned skin and sparkling blue eyes, with shaggy, tousled blond hair. The stark contrast between the guy staring at me and the one who stood in front of me at the senior party tears at me.

"Oh," I finally say.

He swallows.

"I—" I have to clear my throat. "I'm sorry," I add. "For...everything."

He gives me an odd sort of smirk, a look halfway between pity and disgust. "And you think I'll accept your apology?"

I sigh. "No. Not really."

"Good."

He pushes past me, his basket clanking into mine and spinning me around.

"I never meant to hurt you," I call out after him.

He whirls around. "I swear to God, if you keep talking to me, you'll regret it."

Oh. I swallow and nod. He rolls his eyes, his jaw clenched, and turns away again, walking to the front of the store.

I watch him disappear around the corner, and then

have to put out a hand and lean against the shelving. It's funny…how I obliterated everything he stood for, and yet he's the one who somehow moved on, who somehow found himself again, and here I am, still in tattered pieces, putting things together one tiny piece at a time.

It's happening, though. A little at a time, I'm finding myself.

Maybe it helps that I never really knew myself to begin with. I never knew what I wanted, who I was, who I could be. I never took chances, I never spoke up for what I wanted, I never stood out.

It's not like I stood up the first day of college and declared my love for writing. It's not like I stand out yet. But I'm taking baby steps. I'm figuring it out.

The thing is, somewhere along the way, I learned two things.

First, *existing* and *living* are two different things.

And secondly…

Some things can't be undone.

Lies are one of them.

Amber Sheree Photography

About the Author

Amanda Grace is a pseudonym for Mandy Hubbard, author of *Prada & Prejudice* and *You Wish*, romantic comedies for teens. Her first serious novel for teens, *But I Love Him*, was released in 2011. A cowgirl at heart, she enjoys riding horses and ATVs and singing horribly to the latest country tune. She's currently living happily ever after with her husband and daughter in Tacoma, Washington. Visit her at www.amandagracebooks.com.